DARKENED
SOULS

DARKENED SOULS

GARY LEE VINCENT

Burning Bulb

PUBLISHING

Darkened Souls
By **Gary Lee Vincent**

Burning Bulb Publishing
P.O. Box 4721
Bridgeport, WV 26330-4721
www.BurningBulbPublishing.com

Edition ISBN

Paperback 978-0-61593-303-0

First edition.
Printed in the United States of America.

Library of Congress Control Number: 2013922271

Dedicated to:

Anyone who purchased a copy of a *Darkened* novel.

INTRODUCTION

Welcome to *Darkened – The West Virginia Vampire Series Book IV: Darkened Souls*. The book you are now holding represents a reimagining of the vampire mythos in the hellish world of Melas, West Virginia. It could accurately be said that at the conclusion of *Darkened III: Darkened Waters,* I took the characters and story as far as I could go. We basically had an 'end-of-the-world' battle royale mix of Revelation and Armageddon – West Virginia style – all played out on that fateful hillside on Raccoon Run Road. Anything else after that runs the risk of being anticlimactic.

A *Darkened* novel – by design – is intended to create a psychological disturbance in the reader. Thus when setting up a new installment, one must think how to push the envelope just a little bit further than the last one – and go just a little bit deeper than before. Thus, a new direction was in order.

It should be a thrilling experience, I believe, and one that gets you excited, scared, turned on, and desiring to see what happens next.

I do think *Darkened Souls* delivers and am pleased to bring it into 'the fold.' Laugh, cry, but mostly, enjoy the journey into the first installment of the *next* trilogy of terror!

ACKNOWLEDGEMENTS

A *Darkened* book is not a one-man show. With any production that is worth doing right, it is a team effort.

I am extremely grateful for the individuals who supported me on this project. First off, I would like to thank the ever-so-talented Wol-vriey for providing plot support and insight on how we could take the story into new depths, while still keeping the feel of a *Darkened* novel. Similar thanks go out to my content editor Linda Innes for searching out plot holes and keeping the book polished when I veered off track.

Next, I would like to thank my copy editors Teresa Pollack and Rich Bottles Jr. for their making sure my grammar came off well and no major typographical mistakes reared their ugly head in the final.

And last, but not least, thank you, Dear Reader, for sticking with me and supporting freedom of speech and the small press. You are the reason I do what I do.

PART 1

AN OLD BEGINNING

PROLOGUE

The office was almost deserted given the lateness of the evening, the bank of computers standing idle. Almost deserted, but for the elegantly dressed woman seated at one of the desks. She looked too well-dressed, too wealthy and out of place here in this dark open-plan office, gazing vaguely at the screen as she booted up an unfamiliar computer, tapping the keys with her expensively manicured fingers.

The lights were low: just the emergency lights lit, offering a dim glow sufficient to guide people out in case of any incident or accident. Too late. The damage had been done. Hunched over the computer, with the flickering glow of the screen illuminating her hard features, the woman was still silently absorbed in her task. Unseen by her, from the darkness a man's shadow suddenly loomed into view, as his tall body slinked, silently cat-like, through the dimly lit office, until he reached the woman and stood just behind her, his hand twitching to release the object it grasped, pointing it at the back of her head.

"Here is the surveillance video you requested, ma'am," he said, holding out a DVD.

The woman neither flinched nor thanked him. Instead, she slipped the disc into the DVD player and switched it on to play, her eyes greedily searching the images on the screen.

The scenes before her eyes were indescribably shocking. To an untrained eye, these two strangers might have been watching a horrifying snuff movie, because the blood and gore was certainly real, and the plot undecipherable and irrelevant to the violence. But this was not a movie. This was documented evidence of a real-life case.

Lives were being lost before their very eyes, and yet it seemed incredible! Too unreal, somehow, to be true. Men turned against men and women, unaccountable violence in their strange, dull eyes. Monstrous gray-skinned zombie-like creatures, barely human, were seen grabbing and tearing out the throats of terrified people with their bare teeth and claws: some victims dressed as nurses, some wearing nightwear or casual clothing.

Regardless of their dress, blood gushed and spattered and sprayed from arteries, drenching whatever fabric clothed their dying bodies and pooling on the floors. Despite her toughness, even the woman could not disguise a sickened quiver of her lips.

"Are you sure this was not leaked to the authorities?" she asked, her voice firm and authoritative.

"Positive," he replied, appalled but entranced by the scenes playing out on the monitor before him. "That's some really messed up shit on there."

"Don't you mention a word of it outside of here, or I'll personally have your hide," she snapped.

"No, ma'am."

The scenes rolled on across the flat screen on the desk. Both of the viewers knew exactly what they were looking at: the unforgettable bloodbath in Weston State Lunatic Asylum, although few had witnessed these scenes. Few who had remained alive, that is. The seated woman, and the man standing and staring wide-eyed behind her grimly observed the proceedings.

One particular man was striding blindly onwards down the clinical-looking corridor, appearing more human than most of the apparent perpetrators: not so gray of skin, yet still sickly colored, with dead eyes that belied his existence as a living human being.

Behind the bloody chaos playing out onscreen was the sound of people screaming tinnily through the monitor's speakers turned down low. Then, the focus shifted. It was another setting, as if the scenes were taken from a different CCTV camera.

A middle-aged lady in a shocking pink floral nightgown, who had clearly been held in one of the private rooms off the wards appeared to have been bitten or killed. She lay immobile, barely worthy of notice, and but for the garishness of her clothing, she might have simply blended into the rest of the murdered masses.

Later in the footage, it was clear that the building had started flooding. Water gushed through the doors, and apparently up from the cellars.

"That was the day the river broke," the man stated.

"I know that!" the woman barked. "Quit lurking over my shoulder, anyhow."

The man took a rapid step backwards, still staring at the screen.

The overall structure of the hospital building withstood the deluge, but the floodwater eddied around the reception area of the hospital, billowing clouds of blood visible in the murky pools.

Suddenly, the woman at the computer keyboard peered closer to the screen to scrutinize one particular image that the camera was picking up. Jackie noticed that the 'dead' woman in the shocking pink nightgown from earlier in the film suddenly stirred. Her arm moved, then she became alive suddenly and sprang up, her eyes glowing eerily as she worked her way out of the door.

In the almost deserted office, the phone rang, causing the woman to jump momentarily. She clicked the call onto speakerphone, while she stared at the image of the woman.

"Jackie Nixon," she stated.

"Jackie." It was the governor. "What's the verdict?"

The governor had already told her that he wanted "this Melas affair understated". He had to calm public fears and he wanted to know if her company could come up with a story that the public would buy, in order to push the whole affair under the rug. But right now, she was slightly distracted. She paused the DVD, then turned back to the video footage of the apparently undead woman – Cathy Edwards – leaving the hospital of her own free will. She was no longer alive, of that Jackie was certain. She was not a ghoul like the gray, tattered creatures, but a vibrant vampire – fangs exposed, eyes glittering.

"Hold on, governor," Jackie briefly muted the speakerphone and turned to the man in the room. "How's the video rework coming along?"

"We should have enough alternative scenes to make folks think it was a government conspiracy or some kind of Hollywood magic that occurred."

She un-muted the phone, "Governor, if you can assure me that the situation was localized to only north-central West Virginia, then I think we can come up with a believable cover-up for you."

"There are no reports of the zombies, or whatever the hell they were, anywhere else," the governor replied.

"Good. See if you can get the state to reclaim the disaster area and you and I will talk. I have a restoration project in mind."

Jackie clicked off the speakerphone and watched, again, the unbelievable scene of Cathy Edwards apparently coming back to life.

Except, it wasn't life.

CHAPTER 1

Melas had been the venue for the greatest battle of all times: the battle between good and evil. The End Times. Yet, this was only the beginning.

Not many people have ever survived battling against the devil, and if it wern't for the fact that Amanda and William were returned to life by the enigmatic and superhuman Jay Christiano after the final battle, neither of them would have been here to tell the tale.

By some miracle, despite being killed, William and Amanda were now perfectly alive and healthy. Jonathan Harker didn't fare so well. Ironically, it had been a combination of several things that had caused his demise. He was taken to the hospital by Amanda immediately after his broken body had collapsed after a devastating fall down a hillside, and a pitched battle with Lucifer himself. The last straw had been seeing the dead bodies of his adoptive son William, and his beloved Amanda, tossed carelessly aside. He had nothing to live for, he believed. Exhausted and battered, he lost the will to live, and his body gave out as he blacked out into unconsciousness.

He didn't see the restitution that Jay Christiano had made, and the final miracles he performed, driving

Lucifer away and resolving the dreadful ills the devil had done against Jonathan's adoptive family. Jonathan, in his dead faint and close to death himself, had completely missed the inert, breathless bodies of William and Amanda rise magically from the dead. But not as the ghouls and vampires had done, as the walking dead – but as gloriously alive human beings, restored to health by the force of good imbued in Jay Christiano himself. As if waking up from sleep, Amanda and William looked around in surprise and wonder, to see that all signs of the battle had disappeared, except for Jonathan's shattered body.

Jonathan had been critically injured and spent weeks in intensive care in West Virginia, with Amanda by his side, concerned and anxious, holding his cold hand in hers and praying for his life.

"Jon, if you survive – and you have just GOT to survive," begged Amanda, "I swear – I will never leave you."

As if he could hear her pleading even through his medically-induced coma, Jonathan rallied. Day by day, he got a little better, and the doctors swore it must have been divine intervention that helped him. Because by rights, he should have died of his severe injuries.

The surgeon had muttered to the anesthesiologist during his first operation, "Christ only knows how he's still alive!"

And that was true. Only Jay Christiano knew.

When Jonathan pulled through, and was moved to a private room for the start of the months of rehabilitation to regain his mobility after the repair of his shattered bones and burst organs, Amanda often spent the night balanced on the edge of his hospital bed, clinging to his body, or clambering on top of him to perform her own sort of physical therapy.

Before long, Jonathan was out of the hospital, recuperating at home, with Amanda. From a lust that was physical and a friendship and loyalty that had sustained their relationship, they were both in no doubt that they truly loved one another.

Jonathan gazed into Amanda's eyes, unable to believe that this good-looking, sexy woman had stood by him all these months, and kept the faith, staying by his side throughout his ordeal and his upward struggle to regain the use of his body.

"You're incredible," he smiled.

"I am," Amanda nodded. "This is so true. I commend you on your observation."

"So incredible, in fact, that I don't think I'm going to let you go!"

Amanda laughed, "You think I'm going to try to go?"

"Just in case..." Jonathan pulled Amanda by the waist closer to his body, and kissed her lips softly, "I want you to marry me."

Amanda pulled away and looked intently into his eyes, "Seriously?"

"Am I laughing?" Jonathan said, unsure whether or not to be offended.

"If you're serious," smiled Amanda, "Then seriously, I say yes!"

They fell into one another's arms, delighted and relieved to be alive.

Around this time they also found out that Amanda was pregnant. Although they weren't to know what this would mean.

***

Amanda's nephew William, meanwhile, had gone back to Canada to resume his church duties. Amanda had encouraged him to go back to his training as a priest. He was already an incredible young exorcist, and his talents needed to be used.

"But I don't want to leave you – and Johnny..." he began.

"Willy, you need to follow your vocation," she said. "We're fine here. There's nothing you can do – except pray for Jon, and where better to do that than the seminary, surrounded by people like you?"

Reluctantly, reassuring himself that Jonathan was in the best possible place for his recovery, and that Amanda was strong enough for them both, William decided that his battle with evil had reconfirmed his faith and his passion for the Church. So he went back.

Initially, William did not tell the church what had happened but, unable to fully comprehend his own miraculous recovery, or the unbelievable events that had occurred, and after constantly poring over the details in wonder, after a couple weeks he decided to mention his strange experience in the hope of instigating discussion and finding some answers. Every day when he looked in the mirror to shave, he fingered his throat, unable to believe that he had somehow survived having it slashed. More than that – he knew he had died, if only for a short while. He remembered the blackness and cold of the outer darkness, evil demonic forces of the damned ripping and clawing at his flesh, then pleading for help, followed by a white light, and a feeling of supreme calm and peace. And then, as God is his witness, he would swear that Jay Christiano – the modern-day embodiment of Jesus Christ himself – told him it wasn't his time, and sent him back.

His aunt, Amanda, was busy tending to Jonathan, who was still dangerously ill by that stage. William didn't want to bother her by phoning her up and trying to make sense of it all, so he had no one to talk to, and the thoughts whirring in his mind were driving him mad. For one thing, this miracle was bigger than himself. Bigger than Amanda and Jonathan. It had implications for the entire world. Maybe it was his duty to report it. The more he thought about it, the more he remembered a sense that Jay Christiano had saved his life for a specific purpose. It WAS his duty to tell other people. First, he would tell Father Demetrius.

Unfortunately, broaching the issue hadn't got him the support and explanations he craved.

William McConnellson III nervously looked from Father Demetrius Tarrant back to Archbishop Phelps. From the moment he had opened his mouth, he knew they did not believe him.

"So you're saying that you actually met Jesus Christ - or rather, someone claiming to be our Lord - and that he personally helped you to escape the zombie apocalypse? Am I hearing you correctly, young man?" The disbelief in the Archbishop's eyes and the condescending tone of his voice was nothing short of accusatory.

Father Demetrius interjected before William could reply. "He sat right there in my office and claimed a man named Jay Christiano first saved him from most certain death in freezing water during his sabbatical in the States and then saved him once more, just hours later. That 'Good Samaritan' could only have been our Savior, he reckons. Isn't that right, son?"

William swallowed hard. These guys were already starting to misconstrue the report he'd just given after returning from the nightmarish hellhole he had left in West Virginia.

"What I said was, 'I had been killed by a servant of Satan himself and that Jesus Christ had saved me, to return and report what had happened.' That is what I said."

"I see," Phelps replied. "Father Demetrius has a point. You also claimed this Christiano fellow did not say he was Jesus, but in a near death experience, revealed himself to you."

"That is correct."

"Humm..." The Archbishop leafed through some notes on the subject and shook his head. "You also indicated that the Archangel Michael had – how did you put it? 'Possessed' you into participating in the End Times battle?"

"I was used by Michael and my Aunt Mandy was used by Gabriel, to battle the devil."

"Stop right there, son," the Archbishop interrupted. "Demons possess people; angels do not. You need not go any further."

"I agree with the Archbishop," Father Demetrius confirmed. "What you have described in your report is delusional and undeniably fabricated. I would suggest that you seek counseling for…"

"Now you wait a minute, both of you!" William objected. "Neither of you were there! I lived it! My very throat was cut by one of the bastard sons of Satan himself! Who are you to say whether or not it was real?"

"Let me see your scar," Archbishop Phelps calmly asked.

William looked down at the ground. "I don't have one," he said under his breath, almost in a whisper.

"What was that, son?" Phelps made him repeat.

"I said I don't have one!" William yelled out. "Jesus healed me completely that night."

"Even Jesus had the scars from the nails that had been driven into his hands, that he could show, to prove his case to Thomas," Father Demetrius observed.

"Correctly put!" the Archbishop replied, looking over at Father Demetrius to make direct eye contact with the priest. "This young man is definitely making this up. And we abhor lies!"

"I'm not lying!" William cried, desperately.

The Archbishop turned back to William, a tight grimace on his face: "I believe it is in the best interest of the Church that you walk away from the priesthood for a while until you are in a better mental state."

"I am perfectly fine!" William retorted.

The men raised disbelieving eyebrows at one another, which further fuelled William's anger.

"Let us be the judge of that, son," Father Demetrius said, patronizingly waving his hand in a dismissive gesture.

William was incensed. "You wouldn't know the truth if it kicked you in the balls – neither of you!" He reached up and tore off his white collar, flinging it towards the men. "Take this, and your fucking priesthood! I'm out of here!"

CHAPTER 2

SEVEN MONTHS LATER

William tugged back the stiff square of floral curtain that covered the small window of his trailer, and rubbed the condensation off the cold glass to peer out at the gray day outside. Still Canada. Still the concrete and dust road of the trailer park where he'd been living for the last six months. Same old same old. No change, no matter how much he'd hoped and wished for a miracle. But maybe he'd used up all his credit with God. No wonder he needed a drink to get through the day, these days. He rubbed his fingers through his greasy hair and winced against the dim light breaking through the grimy pane of glass. His head was dull and pounding. Again. Like every day, he spent his time stuck in the trailer park, drinking beer and smoking. By day, these habits seemed to settle his nerves, and sooth the ragged pain of anxiety that caught at his chest otherwise, and by night the alcohol left him unconscious, so the nightmares couldn't break through his disturbed mind and scare him shitless.

What he'd gone through would take its toll on anyone. A terrible battle against Satan himself was bad enough, then being killed – his body lying broken and dead and his spirit meeting Jesus! That would freak

16

anybody out. Visiting the afterlife, then being brought back to life – all of this was too much for any young man. For him to carry the burden of this recollection alone had driven him close to the edge. Losing his job, losing his vocation as a priest and losing the support of the Church had tipped him over. Excommunicated! With Jonathan, his father-figure, away in a different country starting a new family with William's only living relative, Aunt Amanda, William felt isolated and more alone than ever.

Jonathan had tried to persuade him to come down and stay with him and Mandy, but William was stubborn. He felt a little put out that Jonathan and his aunt were a tight family unit now, with a baby on the way.

To tell the truth, he was jealous of the baby, getting all that care and attention. Still a teenager himself, William wasn't above wanting a family and affection himself, but to overcompensate for his craving, he pretended he was independent; that he didn't need them. He was quite capable of taking care of himself, he boasted, and was living on his own in a trailer in Canada.

But months had gone by, and his savings had run out. So had his energy and resilience – and his sanity was disappearing, too. Horrifying nightmares robbed him of sleep, and he sought respite by drinking his troubles away. His behavior had become odd – with him manifesting classic symptoms of post-traumatic stress disorder – reliving the trauma, being emotionally numb, and unable to cope; he was drunk much of the time and nobody would give him a job. This was part of the psychological toll of all the stress on his life. He was hitting a new low, and had to face the fact that he had nowhere else to go.

So the next time Jonathan invited William to come down and stay with him and Mandy, he had run out of both money and excuses. But old habits die hard, and he was still no pushover when Jonathan broached the subject of him coming to live with them. His pride wouldn't allow him to relent unless Jonathan practically begged him to come.

"The baby will be here in a couple weeks..." Jonathan began.

"What? And you'll need a babysitter?" William snapped back. "Is that why you want me there?"

"No..." Jonathan lowered his voice in seriousness. "It would be great to have you settled here, and for us to be a family again, before this little stranger appears."

"Hmm," William's tone sounded unconvinced.

"You'll like our house in Morgantown, Willy, and it's good old West Virginia – which you love, anyway."

"Hmm," William grunted non-committedly.

"Hey – you could even enroll at WVU, take some college classes," suggested Jonathan, "and maybe find a new career down here!"

"Mmm."

"Willy, we miss you. It's just not the same without you. We care, and we worry about you. So come over here, where we can care and worry close by instead of hundreds of miles away."

He let Jonathan continue to persuade him. He didn't make it easy for him, reluctant to admit that he actually wanted to come. All the same, William eventually agreed. He had nothing to lose, after all.

"Terrific, Will. I'll send you a bus ticket tomorrow! Are you free, maybe Saturday, to travel?"

"Hmmm. Lemme get back to you," William muttered. "I have to check my planner – see if I have any important business meetings that day."

"Ha ha..." Jonathan said ironically. "So you'll come then?"

"Awww... if you miss me that much, and you're twisting my arm... then, I guess so."

"We do miss you, son."

William's heart swelled with warmth at the word 'son', and he clicked off the phone, an unaccustomed smile stretching his lips for the first time in three quarters of a year.

Summoning up what energy for action he still had available, William packed up his meager belongings and when the bus ticket arrived, it was with a lighter heart and lifted spirits that he left Canada. He was even at the Greyhound station bright and early before 6am for the seventeen hour journey to Morgantown. He found himself actually looking forward to the new adventure.

The long journey gave him a chance to collect his thoughts, sober up, and prepare himself for a whole new life. Now, he had his family back, and things were looking better than ever. The only way was up!

10:30pm in Morgantown, and Amanda was hustling Jonathan to take her to the bus station to pick up Willy.

"I have to come and meet him, Jon!" she swung pleadingly on his arm. "I'm so excited to see him after all this time!"

"Mandy," warned Jonathan. "You better stay home. I don't want Jonathan Junior being born on the freeway!"

"Or Amanda Junior!" She playfully tapped his chest with the palm of her hand. They had not wanted to know the sex of their child; Amanda particularly insisting that she wanted 'to be surprised'.

"Oh, it's a boy! Look at the size of you! That's why you can't fit in the car! We won't be able to get the seat-belt around you!" Jonathan teased.

"Funny guy!" she play-slapped him again. "Cut the crap. I'm coming!"

"All right. I guess I can't argue with the mother of my son."

"Or daughter!" Amanda yelled, grinning. They were both pressing one another's buttons for fun. "And drive carefully, Poppa Bear. There's still surface water on the roads after the rain."

"As long as there's no flooding, we'll be fine," Jonathan winked.

"Or fucking zombies..." Amanda rolled her eyes. At least they could laugh about their trauma these days, now that everything was good again.

She eased herself into the front seat, and they set on their way, laughing and joking, out into the dark of night.

William stood shivering in the doorway of the bus station, listening to the hiss of tires through the rainwater as buses pulled in and out, and cars and cabs dropped by to pick up people. He strained his eyes through the darkness and the occasional beams of headlights, scanning for his own ride. Weird. Jonathan knew the time of his bus – he had bought the ticket, after all. He knew that William would get into Morgantown at 11pm. Okay, so maybe he anticipated there could be some hold-ups, but it was now 11:40 by his watch, and William was freezing out here. He'd tried Jonathan's cell phone a few times, but it rang out, with no response. He was aware that the heavily pregnant Amanda might have stayed at home instead of coming to meet him, so he thought he could maybe catch her by phone, at least. But both Amanda's cell phone and their house phone went straight into voicemail. Nobody was contactable at all by phone. That was all pretty weird.

He waited a few more minutes, puzzled and growing concerned. He was just about to take a cab, when a police car pulled up at the station entrance. William recoiled, feeling unaccountably guilty. Surely he was allowed to loiter at a bus station, waiting for his ride? He took a step back into the shadows, preparing his speech in case he was questioned in any way.

Two uniformed cops got out of the car: a fat guy and a tall, slim female officer. They entered the near-deserted bus station and the fat male officer scanned around. The female officer had already caught William's reluctant eye, and set off towards him.

Oh, crap! he thought. *What have I done now?*

"William McConnellson?" the woman cop asked, a serious look on her face.

"The Third," William added instinctively.

"You have ID, please, sir?"

He took out his wallet and flashed his card.

"Thank you. Do you have an Aunt – Amanda?"

"Yes," William frowned, distinctly uneasy, but this time, not for his own sake. The fat male officer had waddled over and stood silently by his partner's side, looking gravely at William.

"I'm sorry, Sir, but I'm afraid I have to tell you that there's been an accident..."

William's stomach lurched. "What? What's happened?"

"A road traffic accident. Your aunt has been taken to Ruby Memorial Hospital. She's in critical condition, but managed to tell us that you were at the station before she lapsed into a coma. You're listed as her next of kin..."

"Oh, my God!" he cried, appalled, his hand flying to his mouth. "B... but she's okay, right? She'll be okay?" William stuttered. "What about the baby?"

"I'm afraid I can't say, Sir, but we'll take you straight to the hospital now."

William, in a daze, frowned. *Since when did the police offer cab services? What the hell? How bad was this?*

"Jonathan?" he gasped. "What about Jonathan?"

"I'm sorry," the officer said, patting his shoulder lightly. "But the driver of the vehicle was killed instantly. We believe the man was Jonathan Harker according to his driver's license, but we need someone to identify the body to be sure. I'm sorry to ask you at this moment in time, but are you willing?"

"NO!" cried William.

The female officer reeled back on her heels in surprise. "You won't?"

"No…" William sobbed. "I mean yes… I will. If I must. But no, surely – it can't be?" He turned his tear-brimmed eyes to the female officer. "It can't be them. Please – tell me it's not!"

"I'm sorry, Sir," the woman led him gently into the back of the patrol car, and they set off on the longest, most painful journey of William's life.

For the whole of the drive, William prayed to the God he had almost given up on.

"Holy Lord Our God, please forgive my own transgressions. But if you have any pity and compassion, any love for humanity, please let Aunt Mandy and her baby survive! Please! They are pure innocents! Punish me, if you must punish anyone! You have taken Jonathan – is that not enough? Please, oh, God, please let them live!"

The car could not travel fast enough for William. This was worse than any of his nightmares had been. This was real. But it all seemed like too much to take in. Jonathan didn't make it! He would never see him alive again!

"Please stay alive, Mandy! Please fight!" William chanted the words like a mantra in his mind. If only she had as much will to live as he willed her to have!

On arrival at the hospital, panting and desperate, William ran up to the ward he'd been directed to, the police officers trailing behind him.

"Amanda…" he gasped, arriving at the emergency ward, his eyes panic-stricken.

"Wait here, Sir," a nurse said firmly, holding up her hands as if to physically stop him rushing past and searching for them. She went off to notify God knows whom.

William bounced on the balls of his feet, ready to sprint off in whichever direction Amanda lay in, wanting to see her, hold her hand, talk to her, bring her round, make everything well. He drummed his fingers on the nurses' station reception desk, impatient, the moments going by and taking him further and further away from Amanda.

Accompanied by the nurse, a doctor appeared, his face unemotional behind round pebble glasses.

"How is she?" William asked, wild-eyed.

"Mr. McConnellson, please follow me," the doctor held out one arm, his hand directing William towards a room.

"But how is she? Is she awake yet?" William persisted.

"Please... sit down," the doctor gave a tight smile, and nodded towards the plastic-coated low chairs in the small room. William looked around wildly. This wasn't Amanda's hospital room! Where was she?

"I don't want to sit down!" cried William. "Take me to her! How the hell is she? Tell me!"

"I'm sorry. We did everything we could..."

"No-o-o-o!" William whimpered. "She's not...?"

The doctor simply tightened his lips firmly. "I'm sorry. There was nothing more we could do."

"The baby?"

The doctor slowly shook his bowed head, "I'm afraid that both your aunt and her baby died about ten minutes ago..."

"NOOOOOO!" William shrieked.

William grew up fast in the subsequent days. He had so much to organize, with the inquests, funeral arrangements, insurances, wills and the house, and these necessary tasks somehow staved off his emotional reaction, and his own depression for a while. He had something to occupy his mind that was practical and kept him focused, distracting him from his terrible grief. The doctor had advised him not to see Mandy's body or the baby after they'd died. They had been too badly hurt in the crash.

"Rest assured, you would not want to see them. Remember your aunt as she was. It would only distress you to see either of them."

Numbly, William had conceded to the advice. It was bad enough that he had to identify Jonathan's body, and apart from some scratches on his face, he looked mercifully asleep. But the fact that the doctor had warned him not to see his aunt or his tiny cousin just made him fear that their damage had been monstrous – the sight of them unbearable. The possibilities would haunt him for the next few months. He was happy to be guided to a local funeral director by the doctor, who clearly pitied him and seemed to be trying to make up for the fact that he hadn't been able to save his family's life. And since William was in a state of shock and bewilderment, he was happy for any help he could get. He wasn't sure that triple funerals existed before he had to coordinate one, but numbly, he made all of the arrangements and attended the closed casket service, as if in a dream. He even managed to give an impressive personal tribute to his beloved aunt who'd been a mother to him; his beloved Jonathan, who was a father to him, and to the precious unknown baby, who'd turned out to be a boy. It particularly choked him that the small baby, just about ready to be born, had died before he even had a chance to live. William just couldn't bear it.

The next few weeks, William existed in a kind of twilight zone, walking around like a regular guy, yet numb, asleep and detached, like a somnambulist. His mood was so low, he could not fathom its depths. Miraculously, he was too shocked even to resume his drinking habit. He was so sick to the stomach that nausea rose bitterly in his throat at the thought of doing anything like drinking heavily. It turned out that Jonathan and Amanda's wills had both mentioned him. Indeed, everything that they owned: the house they had bought and its contents, a car, and around a hundred thousand dollars, which surprised him. By the time the insurances came through, he would be a rich young man. But this offered him no consolation, since all he had wanted was his family again.

William's depression grew. He wandered the house in a daze, everywhere was reminiscent of Jonathan and Aunt Mandy. Feeling himself spiraling downwards, with rock bottom within sight, William decided that he had to get out of the house, get out into the world, or he didn't know what he would do. So he started visiting bars again, hanging out with real live people instead of his memories, trying to participate in conversations about the latest sports games and news. Strangely, he didn't feel compelled to drink himself insensible. There was nothing to tamp down, apart from his own feelings. He sat drinking steadily this time, knowing that he had faced the worst in his life and had nothing left to lose.

His favorite bar was also the closest to home: Grady's Sports Bar, where he'd become quite a regular.

"Hey, Will!" the bartender, Mike, hailed him as usual, cracking the top off a bottle of Bud without even asking him what he wanted, and sliding his drink down the polished bar for William to deftly catch. It made Will smile, which was a rare enough event, and gave him a feeling of belonging.

These guys are my family now, he thought wryly.

He chatted about sports, which had been quite a feat for him at the start, since he'd never really followed football, baseball or basketball, but watching a few games on the big screen, and sharing some of the animated and ribald chat, he knew enough these days to get by with the guys. Some women had tried to engage him in conversation, too, but they were all super-confident girls who frankly terrified him. He guessed a sports bar wasn't the place to meet the kind of girl he'd be attracted to. If he was attracted to anyone at all. Really, he'd been through so much over the past year, he was still a celibate priest in his head, and that's the way it might stay for a while, as far as he could tell.

One late afternoon, William was sipping at his second Bud, reading the local paper, when a young woman sat next to him.

She slid him a quick, sidelong glance, but looked quite nervous, her slim fingers endlessly wrapping themselves around one another while she waited at the bar. She was not at all the kind of girl who would come drinking alone in a bar, to William's eyes. She was pretty, small and blonde – quite fragile-looking, and wore big dark-framed glasses that looked nerdy but cute on her small-featured face.

"Hi there, what can I get you?" Mike smiled, barely giving her a glance.

"Um… can I get a… er… a… Diet Coke, please?" she asked.

William's gaze met hers and she briefly gave him a shy smile before looking quickly away. She sipped her Coke and cast her eyes towards the door, shifting her gaze back to the bar counter, then looking up hesitantly towards William, perched on his usual bar stool, still reading the paper, but barely able to concentrate for the young woman's sparrow-like hopping from foot to foot and jerky sipping of her drink.

"Um…" she cleared her throat. "Excuse me…."

William realized that she was speaking to him, although her voice was shy and quiet. "I'm sorry, but could you tell me what time it is, please?" Her mouth twisted apologetically, as if she was embarrassed to ask.

"Sure," William smiled. "It's just after four."

"Thank you," she smiled sweetly, "I forgot my watch."

"That's okay," William looked at her closer, appraising her. Damn, she was a cutie!

She swept a stray strand of white-blonde hair from her face with a slim finger, tucking it into the rest of her hair, which was loosely drawn back with a barrette. Glancing back at the door with concern, she again pecked at her Coke, like a nervous bird.

"Waiting for someone?" William asked, just to make conversation. Maybe she had a date.

The girl bit her lower lip and blushed prettily, "My friend said she'd meet me here at 3:30, but I'm late. You haven't seen her, I suppose? Long dark hair, plump – a little taller than me?" She waved her hand about three inches above her head, then tipped her head inquisitively to one side, like a puppy.

William frowned. "No. Sorry. Can't say I have, and I've been here an hour."

"Oh, dear," the girl's forehead furrowed, and she dug into her purse, pulling out a cell phone, which she tapped and read. "Oh, no! She sent me a text saying she can't make it, but I was so concerned about running late, I didn't even think to check my phone! Damn!"

William smiled. "Hey, no worries. I could use some company."

She looked at him frankly, searching his eyes with her big blue, innocent gaze, as if trying to get the measure of him. William found her difficult to read and couldn't quite make out if he'd offended her.

"I mean... Sorry... I don't mean anything by it. It wasn't a pick-up line or anything!" He held up both hands to protest his innocence. He wasn't ever quite sure how to act with girls his own age, although to be fair, she looked a bit older than he was. Although Jonathan Harker had been no slouch with the ladies, and William had spent a great deal of time in his company, he had gone straight from high school to the seminary, so engaging in small talk – or anything – with young ladies had not been on his itinerary.

She laughed, anyway, which was a relief. "Okay," she smiled. "But only if your paper has a crossword in it."

"You like crosswords?" William asked in amazement.

She shrugged. "I'm afraid so... So shoot me."

William grinned in delight. "I do too!"

They both laughed, and the girl held out her tiny hand to introduce herself, "I'm Kate – Kate Kingsley."

"William McConnellson the Third."

Her hand was cool from the cold glass, and felt as small as a doll's in William's broad mitt. He felt a frisson of something. Something stirring. A feeling he'd never had before. But it felt great!

"Well, William McConnellson the Third. Show me what you've got!" She peered over his shoulder, and he blushed furiously. She pulled away and said seriously, "The crossword. Where is it? Have you started it?"

He riffled through the pages of his paper till he came across the appropriate section, and they sat shoulder to shoulder. William's whole body was aware of the proximity of her petite figure. It was as if his arm was on fire where she leant against him. Her perfume was intoxicating, and even her hair smelt floral and fragrant. As she leant over to peer at the puzzle, he was conscious that her soft breasts pressed against his arm, and he felt himself suddenly aroused.

He bought her another drink and they continued chatting. Kate was a computer technician and once William had overcome her shyness, they hit it off big time. She was gazing into his eyes, making lots of eye contact, smiling and laughing, and touching his arm, sending electrifying signals to his brain. He had goosebumps, as well as a hard-on. As the bar began to get crowded as the evening wore on, William was already head over heels in love.

Kate gazed into his eyes for a long time, smiling inanely, her elbows on the bar, and her pixie chin propped on her elegant hands.

"What?" William asked, feeling silly with beer and love.

"You're so cute!" smiled Kate.

William blushed furiously. "So are you! I mean. I'm not! Not as much as you are!"

She placed her cool hand on his, and curled her fingers under his palm. She began to stroke the center of his palm, sending throbbing impulses directly to his cock. Then her fingers began to caress the skin in between his fingers and his eyes widened. This was the most erotic experience of his life! And they were still in the bar!

"I like you, William McConnellson the Third," Kate said, the tip of her tongue poised between her pink lips, driving William wild. "Do you live nearby?"

"Yes..." William gasped, "just around the corner."

Kate smiled shyly, "I'd like to see your... place. Besides, it's getting crowded in here."

"Yes," William slipped off the stool, uncertain whether he could manage to walk across the bar without his wood being evident to all. He grabbed his jacket and draped it across his arm, hoping to disguise it, provided he didn't walk like something out of Monty Python.

Outside, she slipped her arm through William's comfortably, and they chatted amiably for the couple of blocks until they arrived at William's new home.

William was about to show her around, as she'd suggested, but he pretty soon realized that Kate had been talking metaphorically. Because no sooner had he closed the front door behind them than she stood on her tiptoes and pressed her open mouth against his. And he was lost.

She entwined her arms around his neck and wrapped her legs around his waist so that his throbbing cock was pressed hard against her crotch. He groaned into her wide open mouth, panicking that he would shoot his load right there and then.

As if she sensed this, Kate lifted herself up to his waist and breathed into his ear, "The bedroom, Will. Show me your bed."

He obliged, and carried her feather-light weight into the bedroom, where she slowly undressed him, as he undressed her with trembling fingers. He wasn't sure whether or not he should tell her this was his first time, but because he was embarrassed to admit it, he decided to wing it and see what happened. Consequently, he had no qualms about plunging straight in, unaware of the etiquette of foreplay and finesse. Within three strokes, especially with the sound of Kate's throaty cries of delight, he had erupted into her, so excited he was unable to contain himself. But whether Kate was easily satisfied, trying to encourage him, or being polite, she made out that he was hot stuff, nonetheless.

"Oh, God," she said. "Will! You're amazing!"

"Thank you," Will said, gasping for breath, unable to believe what had happened. "You are... incredible! I have no words!"

She lay with her head lightly resting in the crook of his shoulder, and she talked about her family: her mom and dad were dead, like his, and the more she talked, the more comfortable he felt with her. He confessed that he was all alone in the world, too, and explained the terrible accident that had befallen the last two people he'd had in the world. Kate had sat up in surprise, and shed a tear on his behalf, kissing away his tears as they fell, and nestling his head in her bosom as he cried. Kate told him all about her job, which wasn't very interesting, but William hung onto her every word, finding her fascinating. She stopped chattering and turned to him.

"You haven't told me about your job."

"I don't have one at the moment." He cleared his throat, embarrassed. "I... actually, I used to be a priest."

Kate leant up on her elbow and said in surprise, "Really? Oh, my God!" Then she covered her mouth with her hand and laughed nervously. "Sorry to blaspheme! I'm just surprised!"

"Yeah," William said wryly. "So am I."

"Oh, my God – I just fucked a priest?"

William started, embarrassed. "Sorry if I... if... er... This. I... went into the seminary early. I was barely a teenager. So I'm not very... well, not at all. What we did...I... you are my first."

"I mean," she said, "I'm surprised that, for a virgin, you're actually pretty great!"

A red blush crept from William's cheeks down his throat and across his chest.

"And practice makes perfect," she said, clambering on top of him.

CHAPTER 3

West Virginia Governor Tyrone Brown was a squat, fat, man. He had balding hair, a squashed nose, and thick lips. He was efficient at running his state, with just the right balance of pragmatism and ruthlessness in his character makeup to make him a good governor.

The one thing Governor Brown hadn't planned for on becoming governor of West Virginia was ulcers.

"They're an occupational hazard, Ty," his wife Betty always said while he protested and drank more than the prescribed dose of Mylanta. "You've a nervous disposition. You'll only stop ulcering when you leave office."

"I'm quite likely to leave office in a hearse," Tyrone always retorted. "Thank God my heart's strong. What is wrong with people? It's like they exist simply to make the governor's life hell. No matter what you do, someone's always pissed off. Someone always wants something more. And usually for the most bizarre reasons."

Betty shrugged. "Well you know the old saying, 'He who pays the piper dictates the tune.'"

"I'm tired of dancing," the Governor retorted.

35

***

The current situation of Jackie Nixon wanting to buy the town of Melas was what was activating Tyrone Brown's ulcers.

Jackie Nixon... George Nixon's wife.

George was a Texas billionaire, he practically bled money. His family owned so much oil-rich land that they were virtually royalty.

George and Tyrone were old friends. They went way back, had attended Yale together – Tyrone on a scholarship, George because... it was family tradition. You were born, you went to Yale, you graduated, got slotted somewhere in the family business, got married to a ditzy blonde who in turn gave birth to the next son that attended Yale.

Only in this case, all hadn't gone totally to plan. God had handed Jackie and George a daughter – not son – to look after. It looked like the male succession ended with George, unless grandchildren counted.

George Nixon had no real interest in politics. The amount of money he had, however, meant politicians were desperately interested in him. George was ceaselessly being lobbied by Washington's political elite for his support in their electioneering.

He had, for instance, been instrumental in securing the Democrat's West Virginia governorship ticket for Tyrone Brown, and spent a substantial amount of money funding his campaign. And now, it looked quite possible that a Senate bid was in his future, after his term in the governor's chair.

George had never asked Tyrone for anything in return for his political support. Until now.

"But you can't simply buy a *town!*" Tyrone had sputtered into the phone a week ago, when George had told him Jackie's intent.

The billionaire's aged voice croaked over the line with its thick southern drawl. "Why not, Ty? The state practically *stole* the town from all of the property owners via eminent domain after FEMA declared it a no-man's land. So technically, the *State of West Virginia* owns the town now, so the way I figure, if you own it you can sell it. You know and I know that no one wants the fucking place. Except... Jackie."

"What does she want it for?"

"Who gives a shit? Just fuckin' let her have it, for God's sake."

"George, *everyone* in the state will give a shit. Remember the taxpayers? The damn press and their 'people have a right to know' bullshit? I'll be run out of the state."

George laughed, "Yeah. They'll railroad you out of town for sure. Tar and feathers galore – you'll be so covered in feathers, you'll look like one of Colonel Sander's birds." He paused and coughed. "Okay, I get you. Jackie says she wants to use the town for a health resort/spa – a place for women with too much money to congregate and plan their world dominion. How's that?"

Tyrone sighed. "Both you and I know that won't wash with the state planning and developmental committees. We're not going to sell her Melas for that reason."

"That's what I thought, too."

"George, the biggest problem with selling Melas at the moment is what happened there. Any other patch of countryside and you could just buy up the property and own it. Since the flood however, with the burst dam and all, media scrutiny has been so acute on everything we do, it's like I'm Saddam Hussein dodging NASA spy satellites."

George chortled. "It's that bad, eh?"

"It's worse than that. The fucking Republicans in the Legislature are just waiting for a juicy revelation to boot my ass out of office."

There was silence on the other end of the line for a minute. Tyrone could practically hear the wheels of thought spinning in his friend's mind.

When George Nixon resumed speaking, it was slowly, deliberately. "Hmmm. Okay, how about... if it's for a research foundation? You can paint it like Jackie's setting up a memorial charity to commemorate the victims of the Melas flood disaster... Rebuilding... dam research... scholarships... some bullcrap like that. Will your guys buy that?"

Tyrone thought a moment. "That might work."

"Please *make it* work, Ty. Dress it up anyhow you like. Jackie's been getting on me for a month now, to get on you over this. You've got ulcers? I've a bad heart. I've had two heart surgeries, have a pacemaker, and my doctors all tell me to take it easy. The one thing I don't need is a blonde with unresolvable anger management issues hovering around me like an Air Force bomber." He laughed. "It's dumb that I love her."

Ty sympathized. George Nixon was seventy-two, his wife Jackie forty-five. And yes, he did love her. And she was obviously capitalizing on that now.

"I'll see what I can do," he said. "I can't promise..."

"Ty, this is in *both* our best interests. If you don't make this deal happen and get Jackie her pet town and off my neck, I'll be dead before it's time for you to be re-elected. And you can be certain Jackie will do everything possible to ensure you don't get back into the Governor's mansion after your term expires."

Tyrone considered that. He realized George wasn't joking. "I'll try my hardest. It'll cost you an arm and a leg, though."

"Whatever. I'll spend the fucking money to buy my peace of mind. Just convince your people to sell it and convince the press it's a good deal for the state. Thanks, old friend."

George Nixon had hung up. Tyrone sat thinking for a while after. Melas was a pariah town now. A dump. In the aftermath of the flooding and fires that had destroyed the place, and the explosions that had reopened the ancient mine, Melas was such an eyesore now that the Planning and Developmental Commission had proposed blocking the road off, both for aesthetic (tourist) and safety reasons – their geologists suspected that the flooding had weakened the town's substructure and with the mines in the area, sinkholes were a distinct possibility.

It was going to cost an untold amount of money to ever make Melas useful/livable again.

The state didn't want the fucking place. No one did. No one except Jackie Nixon. And as far as the West Virginia governor was concerned, she could have it.

***

Just like Tyrone had told George would be the case, the planning guys resisted the proposal to sell.

The meeting when the Governor had advanced the Nixon proposal was like fighting the American civil war all over again.

"The town *will* be rebuilt," Duncan Smith, Head of Strategic Planning, insisted. "We'll find the money somewhere." Duncan's mother was from Melas. He had lots of relatives buried in the town's cemetery and didn't want to see it turned over for commercial exploitation. "I don't care if she wants to build a hospital on the site," he insisted. "Public property shouldn't be sold to private individuals."

Frida Higgins, Tyrone's blonde head of finance, had scoffed, "Find what money somewhere?" "Duncan, rebuilding Melas will cost close to a billion dollars. We *don't have* that money." Knowing his family connection, and not liking Duncan much, Frida drove the spike in: "No one is going to spend a billion dollars to renovate some hick town no one in the state knows exists."

Duncan wasn't cowed. He shot Frida a cold glare. "If the state managed its money better we'd be have enough."

Frida was extremely stingy with the state's resources and by accusing her of squandering West Virginia's money, the Head of Strategic Planning had just committed the unforgiveable sin. Frida reddened under her makeup, and Tyrone cringed. He *knew* what was coming.

He felt his ulcer start acting up, so he called his secretary, Maria Morales, over. "Get me my antacid tablets and some water," he told her.

"I'll explain where West Virginia's money goes," Frida said testily, beginning her retort to Duncan's accusation over her money-management skills. Tyrone considered stopping Frida's outburst, but didn't dare. If he interrupted her, she'd be mad and take it out on him when he later needed her to approve financing for something essential. She'd most likely insist that the state no longer had the money to fund some slum reconstruction or other.

"There are currently *three* major drains on the taxpayers' income at the moment…" Frida barked.

Tyrone tuned her out. He stared intently at her, nodding occasionally, but in reality, his mind was elsewhere. *There has to be a way,* he thought, *a way to convince this lot to sell Jackie her damn town. Frida will be glad if we sell it. It just means more money in the state's coffers for her to hoard. But Duncan?*

Maria brought Tyrone his medicine and water. While taking the pills, he was forced to listen to his cabinet again.

"It's a ghost town," Frida was stating with obvious glee.

"It's... it's . . ." Duncan stuttered, then fell silent. Tyrone wondered what Frida had said while he wasn't paying attention to them that had made Duncan look cowed, defeated.

Everyone else around the table was following Tyrone's lead, letting Frida vent her anger. Duncan should have known better, they all reasoned. You didn't accuse Frida of financial mismanagement and live happy ever after.

"*It is* a ghost town," Frida said, blonde head bobbing furiously. "From your own accounts, Melas had been practically deserted for two years... even before the flood." She smiled at Tyrone, who was once again lost in thought. She mistook his smile for assent and continued: "I don't really understand your resistance to this sale. If we were talking about a place with *value*, for instance..."

Duncan just stared gloomily waiting for today to end.

In the end it was Shelly Vining, Tyrone's legal adviser, who'd resolved the matter. Like her boss, she'd ignored Frida's tirade, her mind on how to offload Melas in a way acceptable to everyone seated. Finally, Shelly had worked it out. She didn't immediately interrupt Frida, however, not because she was scared of repercussions, but because she enjoyed watching Duncan writhe with embarrassment. She thought Duncan a fatuous jerk, so she was disappointed when Frida stopped and sat down, her eyes daring Duncan to make a comeback.

To his credit, Duncan would have. He sputtered, about to retort. Shelly, however, cut him off. Twice defeated, Duncan subsided back into his seat, unwilling to have his head handed to him on a plate again.

"I've worked it out, Mr. Governor," Shelly said.

"Yes?" Tyrone said expectantly, unable to think up anything himself.

"It's simple really," Shelly said. "We'll sell Melas to Jackie Nixon, only we won't sell it to her."

There were excited buzzes around the table. "How do you mean?" Tyrone asked.

Shelly smiled. "We'll let Jackie spend the money we don't want to spend rebuilding Melas for us, and then we'll use a legal loophole to snatch it back from her. This way we get paid twice."

The cabinet murmured. Tyrone raised a concerned eyebrow.

"So Jackie is essentially paying the state for the privilege of repairing the town for us?" Frida said, "All told, a loss of close to two billion dollars for the Nixons?"

"Yeah," Shelly replied.

"I like it," Frida smiled. "They're too rich by far. Their tax payments should be more closely investigated by the IRS."

"I like it too," Duncan admitted. "But what loophole will you use?"

Shelly frowned at Duncan so he knew she wasn't siding with him, then turned and smiled at Tyrone. "I'll insert several small clauses that will give us the power to reclaim Melas if she defaults any of them. Then we'll ensure that she does default."

Everyone else nodded their assent. Tyrone was the only one who caught the slight wink Shelly had given him, meaning he should not worry – Melas would actually be sold to Jackie Nixon for good.

The governor rose to his feet. "Meeting's over for today. Frida and Duncan?" The warring pair looked at him enquiringly. "Both of you get to work on the valuation of the town. Wring as much money from the Nixons as we can. We want top dollar for that…" Tyrone almost said 'dump' then remembered Duncan's sensitivity about Melas, "… place."

The pair nodded. Tyrone turned to Shelly, "Shelly, please wait so we can talk this over some more. Everyone else, we'll get across to you with the details."

With everyone pleased, the West Virginia state executive cabinet dispersed.

"You know there'll be hell to pay if we double-cross the Nixons, don't you?" Tyrone asked Shelly when they were all alone.

Shelly Vining crossed her legs and smiled, "We're not double-crossing them, sir. I just had to tell everyone something, else we'd be here till the cows come home."

She brushed brown hair out of her face, her grey eyes stared coolly into Tyrone's faded blue ones. "Calming Duncan down was essential, sir. Without him, the deal doesn't go through."

Shelly was right. Tyrone grimaced. "That damn brother of his."

Duncan's elder brother Dan owned the Charleston Chronicle, the state's most respected newspaper.

Shelly nodded, "One word about any hanky-panky in the Capitol, and you'll be up for impeachment."

Tyrone nodded, "Thanks, Shelly." His face winced with thought. "But how do we keep from really duping the Nixons now that everyone *knows* that's the plan?"

"That's easy. Small print stuff, legalese. After putting in all the buyback clauses, we'll insert an overriding clause stating that buyback only comes into effect if Jackie defaults in paying half the sum in the next three months. Which she obviously won't."

"Hmmm... good," Tyrone said. "It's still a little light, though. Make it tighter. George is a good friend of mine. I don't want to see him accidentally get the short end of the stick. What happens if for instance, the Chinese default on some loan repayment, and Washington has another recession and he can't move his money around in time to pay?"

Shelly nodded. She thought a moment. "I've a solution for that, sir. Our legal departments will insert a failsafe into the contract ensuring that in any unforeseen circumstances we can't buy Melas back from Jackie Nixon for the next sixty years or so. We'll camouflage it deep in the small print. If it ever gets discovered, we'll regretfully explain it as a clerical oversight."

Tyrone laughed, immediately feeling his ulcer let up. Today was going to be a good day, after all.

"Ha, ha, ha!" he chuckled, slapping his knee in mirth and relief. "You're a total genius, woman. Sixty years? By then it'll be too late for anyone to care about Melas anyway."

"Yes, sir. We'll all be long dead and buried."

CHAPTER 4

William was very conflicted. Ever since he'd walked out of the priesthood/seminary, his crisis of faith had only worsened with each day.

William's current life made little sense to him. Everything that had gone before – the Melas Armageddon – seemed a mere dream. He understood that it was impossible for it to be otherwise; even the most cataclysmic event loses its ferocious intensity as time goes by. But it must leave a clear effect in its wake. What bothered William most, however, was his own behavior.

I met Jesus Almighty in the flesh, and he raised me from the dead. And next thing, I ditch the seminary because my teachers don't believe me? I lose my temper for five minutes and ditch a lifetime of belief? Would I have believed it if I hadn't actually experienced what happened in Melas with the vampires?

And then, what next? I start drinking, smoking pot occasionally, and now I'm sleeping with a woman I'm not married to. Just great, William! Where is thy faith? You meet the Son of God and next thing you know, you go downhill. Somehow, I think you're supposed to ascend rather than descend.

William had at first felt guilt about screwing Kate. But the longer they'd been in love, the more sex they had, the more his initial conviction of the wrongness of their actions had faded, drowned in the ocean of pleasure that Kate's body gave him. And now?

Now, I revel in her body, I can't get enough of her sensuous flesh.

He grinned, though oddly, he was certain he should be crying, that he'd thrown away something priceless; as Christ put it – he'd 'cast his pearls before swine.'

Try as he might, no matter how drunk or doped he got, William couldn't shake the feeling that his creator was very pissed off at him and that this, his current extended sabbatical and lapse of faith would shortly come back to bite him deeply in the ass.

***

Kate walked into the living room, toweling her blonde hair dry.

She kissed William, then picked up the TV remote. "Where do we go tonight?" she asked while surfing channels.

"Let's go see *Mindspores*, that new Donald Jackson movie."

Kate wrinkled her nose. "Okay, but you're one up on me. It's chick flick next time."

"So long as it's not Julia Roberts…"

"Sshh," Kate said, pointing to the TV.

William looked bemusedly at the screen. It showed two people, a man and a woman, standing in front of a podium at the top of a terrace of steps, surrounded by a mob of journalists. The camera zoomed in for a close up.

"That's West Virginia governor Tyrone Brown," William said. He pointed to the woman besides the governor, a beautiful middle-aged blonde who looked like a politician's wife. "But that isn't his wife. Who's she?"

"Jackie Nixon," Kate said disgustedly. "Possibly the richest bitch in America."

"You clearly don't like her," William observed.

"There's *nothing to like* about her," Kate said with angry conviction. "She and her husband George Nixon bleed the poor to feed the rich."

"I thought that was the government's job," William said. He remembered George Nixon now, an aged shriveled man. "That's his wife? She's much younger..."

"She's a gold-digger, that's all. And now she's bought an entire town to dig gold out of!"

"You sound like you've had personal expe..."

William froze and shut up. He'd just made sense of the red banner splashed across the bottom of the screen: 'Sale of Melas to Jackie Nixon approved by West Virginia State Legislature.'

William sat bolt upright. "Kate, did you just say she bought a town?"

Kate didn't answer. Instead, she unmuted the TV. The scene had meanwhile cut to a TV studio, with Governor Brown and Jackie Nixon inset in a corner rectangle.

A lady reporter was speaking: "In this utterly unprecedented decision by the West Virginia State

Legislature, the town of Melas is, henceforth, private property. Reactions have so far been varied, a high proportion of them negative." She frowned, "I have here with me Professor Joseph Rudin of the West Virginia Institute for Socio-Environmental Studies. Hello, professor, and welcome to the program."

The camera centered on Professor Rudin, a thin dour man in a dark green suit. He smiled coolly. "Thank you, Mary."

"Now, professor, can you please enlighten the viewers as to what this means for state and national politics?

"Well, as you're well aware," Professor Rudin began, "many people are alarmed by this sale, believing it will pave the way for other billionaires to begin buying up towns all over the country, possibly even this one, Charleston, our state capitol."

He laughed. "I doubt it will ever come even close to that." His expression became serious, like he was addressing a classroom of students. "But... public apprehension is understandable, though our concerns are *misplaced*. The sale of Melas is actually of immense benefit to the state–"

"Forgive me for interrupting you, professor, but how is selling a town beneficial?"

"Well for one thing, it provides the state with a one billion dollar injection of cash into our anemic financial system. Governor Brown says he's already earmarked half this sum for improving our health care system, with special emphasis on..."

"Turn it off," William told Kate. "They're mad."

She muted the TV. The scene had once again changed to show Jackie Nixon and the governor in close-up. The impact of Jackie's beauty – her high cheekbones, full lips, and deep blue eyes – was all lost on William.

"Wow," Kate said, like she was reading his mind. "She looks like a plastic surgery advertisement." Her apparent ability to know what he was thinking was one of the things William most loved about Kate.

"They're all mad," William repeated. "Melas is an *evil* place; somewhere best left to rot."

"Not anymore," Kate said. "Mrs. Moneybags is about rebuilding it."

Onscreen, Jackie Nixon smiled for the cameras.

"She has absolutely no idea what she's buying," William said. "She'd have been better off losing the money on the stock market or flushing it down a toilet."

Kate came and sat next to him on the sofa. "Okay, darling, I think it's time for your big confession. What really happened in Melas?"

"I told you…"

"A made-up story. Don't look so surprised, William. I've never believed your 'found-an-old-Templar-relic-and-had-an-out-of-body-experience-and-met-Jesus' tale. It's so obviously made-up! They don't kick people out of the priesthood for that shit. I mean, the Church thrives on…"

"They *didn't* kick me out, remember? I quit."

"But why? Because you had a vision of Jesus? That makes no sense. Why quit *after* actually seeing the Messiah? That story sucks." She frowned, "I've always known there was something you were hiding. I never asked before because I could see it was something that had really hurt you and I didn't want to re-open old wounds. I love you too much to want to hurt you." Kate smiled sadly, peering intently into his eyes. "What did happen, darling?"

"You would never believe me," William said. "Not in a million years."

"William, I fucking love you," Kate said, shades of anger creeping into her voice. "I've remained with you this long, knowing you were hiding some big secret from me. Just tell me what the fuck happened back there in that town!" She calmed, adding, "It's important to me because it's important to you."

He shook his head. "You won't believe me."

"Just tell me," Kate said coolly. "Let me decide if you're a credible witness or not, okay?"

William saw she was serious. So he told her all about Melas and Victor Rothenstein and the vampires, the ghouls, and the barely averted mini-apocalypse.

Onscreen, Jackie Nixon waved to the assembled reporters. She shook hands with the governor, then descended the steps of the West Virginia state house and entered a white stretch limo. It drove off in a popping of flashbulbs. The scene cut back to Mary Riley and Professor Rudin, then to an advertisement for Mylanta antacid.

"Wow," Kate said, when William was done speaking. "If I didn't know you like I do, I'd have thought you were an acidhead."

"You see," William said glumly, "I warned you that you wouldn't..."

"But I do believe you," Kate said earnestly. She took both of William's hands in hers and stared deep into his eyes. "I *do* believe you, darling. I'm not saying that I understand how anything you've described could have possibly happened, but I can see in your eyes and hear in your voice that you're not lying." She suddenly laughed and pointed at the TV. "Ha hahahahahahahaha!"

"What's funny?" William asked.

A photo of Jackie Nixon was onscreen. Kate managed to stop laughing. "I'm just thinking that she deserves whatever happens to her in Melas. Vampires, eh? A social leech like Jackie Nixon deserves to have all the blood sucked out her."

William smiled. The TV switched to a state infomercial. William sat and watched the silenced ad for continuing education programs at West Virginia University.

His primary feeling now was of intense relief. *Kate believes me. I finally have someone to share the full burden of my past life with. So what if all those faggy old seminary professors think I'm–* He cautioned himself. *Don't even THINK that.*

"Forget going out to the movies," Kate said suddenly. "Let's go make love."

"Huh? But I really want to see *Mindspores*."

Kate rolled her eyes. "Tomorrow. Right now you look so stressed that only a good fuck will heal you."

She pulled up her skirt. "Look... no panties."

William grinned at the exposed blonde thatch at the junction of her thighs. He got up and followed her into the bedroom.

CHAPTER 5

Alison Smith peered warily out of the front door of her prefabricated cabin.

Wary. That was the only word, in Alison's mind, that accurately described how she felt while looking out of a perfectly normal door into the brilliant sun-lit mid-morning. It was a lovely day. Alison had no reason to be bothered, yet she was. Badly so. She felt like she stood beneath a storm cloud about to break.

Alison Smith was forty-seven; a short brunette; plump, but not overly so, and passably pretty. She was a mousy, inconspicuous woman; a bookworm of a nervous disposition, more at home in a library than in a gathering of people. She liked being unnoticed.

There's nothing out there, Alison told herself. *Stop being a scaredy-cat.*

There are memories here, a ghostly thought contradicted her. *Memories best left alone.* The thought, an ineffable consideration, gone almost before Alison realized she'd thought it, had sounded female.

It had also sounded *dead.*

Alison stepped out into the sunshine, spooked now despite her best attempts not to be.

Stop this, she thought angrily. *It's superstition, nothing more. You're letting yourself be affected by what you know happened here.*

It wouldn't do to let her work run her life.

She looked around the work camp. The neat rows of prefabricated cabins laid over concrete reinforced her firm belief that logic and not the paranormal was the controlling force in her life.

She knew this to be true. So why did she still feel something was wrong?

Alison Smith was Senior professor of Occult Studies at West Virginia University. She was well-liked by both her colleagues and her students; the latter of which considered her to be a hip, witchy-woman whom they could relate with and talk to on their level, instead of the oldie-moldy professors in the economics department.

Alison had initially begun studying the occult due to a fascination with ancient Native-American burial rites. She was also well-versed in European Pagan rituals and sometimes wore their symbols as jewelry to keep her in favor with her students. Privately, that interest had transformed into a fascination at the degree of self-deception humans were capable of in their quest for God.

Alison had ceased believing in God or the supernatural during her teen years. She'd substituted rebellion against, or belief in, the unseen for rebellion against parents and authority.

In the beginning of her atheism, Alison had been outspoken, brusque and cynical about religion. Then, the mere hint of 'faith' in those she encountered had made her pout in disgust and spew a tirade of scornful retort.

Over the years, however, her cynicism had softened. It was hard to encounter so much religion and not be affected by it. If Alison wasn't touched by the deities people worshipped, then she was touched by the people who worshipped them – by their sincerity of belief, however misguided it might be. The very fervency of emotion believers possessed was contagious.

Only recently, while outwardly still championing agnosticism and atheism, Alison had begun to wonder if there really might be something or someone out there.

And that had been before she and Don had come to Melas.

**

Don had come home from work two months earlier, all beaming with smiles.

Donovan Smith was a tall, thin, handsome man with sand-colored hair. He was as gregarious as his wife was reserved.

"We got the job!" he enthused at Alison, once done kissing her good evening.

"The contract to rebuild Melas?"

Don nodded his head enthusiastically. "Yes! Yes! The state gave it to Moran-Smith."

"That's wonderful," Alison said, swept up in his emotion.

"This calls for a celebration," Don said. He got out a bottle of champagne, popped the cork.

"Watch the carpet," Alison yelped as the bubbles spewed out of the bottle.

Don laughed. "A toast," he proposed, "to a rain of filthy lucre."

Alison giggled. "I'll drink to that."

Later that night, unable to sleep, Alison got out of bed. Don was snoring gently, his handsome face wreathed in a smile that suggested he was dreaming of making money.

Alison walked across the room to stand naked by the bedroom window. The moon was high in the sky. The slight wind blew into the bedroom, caressing her body, stiffening her nipples like Don's lips had done when they'd made love earlier.

Alison gazed out of the window of their hotel room on Route 50 in Clarksburg toward the direction of Melas. A smile played over her lips. Moran-Smith Architecture getting the nod to redesign Melas was a massive break for her, as well.

A fortuitous one. Melas was perfect for her research.

Alison was writing a book: *Superstition in the Modern Age*. She intended it as an expose of the bogus spirituality most Americans found impossible to let go. She was fairly confident that the university would also approve it to be used as a textbook in her classes on the occult, which was the perfect reason for moving the project forward.

Melas, with its rich culture and tradition of the supernatural, had been one of the towns she'd earmarked to visit and study.

But then the flood/fire/disaster had occurred and the town was declared off limits. Alison had put her book on hold.

And now... *Ha haha!* She grinned. With Don overseeing the town's reconstruction, she could go wherever she liked there; do whatever she wanted.

Whilst looking out over the West Virginian night, in her mind, Alison began drafting her application for sabbatical leave from the university.

Oh, yes, she thought. *I am fucking accompanying Don to Melas and staying there for as long as it takes to get my book right.*

***

But now...

Alison looked over the prefabricated buildings forming the construction company's site. They were laid out in regimental regularity, the precision of their construction testament to Moran-Smith's mastery of aesthetics.

It was noon. Don had left for work at the crack of dawn – he and the team were conducting surveys on the site of the old Melas Community College, mapping the rise and fall of the ground to determine what building outlay would work best. Most of the campus had been destroyed except for the main hall, which set on a small knoll overlooking Main Street. The bottom floor of the structure was completely ruined by the flood, but the library on the second floor, for the most part, remained unharmed.

"Mrs. Nixon has said we can spend what we like," he'd said last night. "And by damn, I intend to. We'll make the new Melas the showpiece of this fucking state."

Alison locked her cabin door. Wearing a light, flower-patterned cotton dress, a straw hat, and open sandals, and carrying her laptop and a sheaf of notes in hand, she walked briskly down the street of uniform dwellings. But for the laptop, she knew she looked like a farm girl off to milk cows.

She waved to those wives she knew as she passed their cabins. All smiled back at her.

It's great to be the boss's wife, Alison thought. She grinned. Hilary Moran, the other 'boss's wife,' had a house full of kids to look after and thus only came around on weekends. Donovan and Alison had never had any children. Both had been too busy to have them when they were young, and now time had run out on them. Or maybe, Alison occasionally thought, they'd gotten into the habit of being alone.

Hilary was a sexy effervescent redhead who consistently had Alison feeling insecure, so she was glad she was hardly ever around. Hilary's husband Mike – the other half of Moran-Smith Construction and Engineering, Inc. – was out with Don.

Alison reached the end of the prefab cabins. From here on back was concrete wasteland – heaps of burnt rubble and girders, bulldozed when the camp was built to clear space for the cabins. Beyond the expanse of rubble was a field of green grass with interspersed trees. With the exception of a large oak at the rear of the expanse, these trees looked to Alison like they had been planted just in the last few years. Beyond that, a wire fence bordered a main road, the other side of which was abandoned farmland, more trees and grass. A pleasant enough place except for the bulldozed rubble.

Alison was headed for the particular ancient oak a short distance from the end of the ruins. She'd made it her workplace – her outside office – whenever she wished to take advantage of the June sun, like today. She'd set up a plastic table and chair under the tree, because it felt nice to work to the chirping of birds and rustle of squirrels.

Yesterday, she'd been out photographing graves. One in particular had caught her attention. It belonged to Walter Pinkman, an antiques dealer, who'd died of a stroke according to public records, but some folks alluded to talk that the old man dealt in more than antiques, but never gave Alison anything more specific. *Fortunately for Mr. Pinkman*, Alison thought, *he died before the real devastation hit Melas.*

* * *

The Moran-Smith camp was built on the site of the old Melas Industrial Home For Troubled Youth. The Home, an institution for delinquent teens, had burnt to the ground in odd circumstances four years previously, and Alison had heard wonderfully delicious tall tales of those circumstances. All of which she intended including in her book as the chapter: 'Reimagining the Truth, Superstitious Mind Point-of-View'.

Skeptic that she was, Alison had been intensely amused by a particular strain of rumors, tales of a huge non-human skeleton found amidst the building wreckage by the firemen – a body quickly spirited away by the government.

Yeah, right. She chuckled now. *Supernatural my foot. It's fucking outrageous the things people think up to explain out-of-the-ordinary happenstances. True, it was sad so many kids died, but, it wasn't monsters, guys—just some pissed-off teen with matches and a can of gasoline.*

Wow, what bullshit folks were prepared to believe!

Still amused, Alison walked over the floor of what she'd been told was the juvenile institute's auditorium – at least what remained of it. The concrete floor survived the fire, along with some of the masonry elements of the building. Different rooms were clearly delineated by the nubs of worn-down wall, while door spaces were marked by their lack of jutting masonry. It had been a long building, and Alison was crossing it at an angle. She stepped between two massive piles of rusted corrugated sheeting and over the foot-high concrete separation into the adjoining room, a medium-sized enclosure.

All of a sudden, the weather turned cold. A wind struck up from somewhere and blew through the concrete graveyard. Alison instantly regretted wearing such a flimsy dress. She looked up. The sun still shone as brightly as before.

So why?

She looked down again, and then turned to her right as she sensed motion there.

Alison gasped. There was a woman standing there. A transparent woman. Alison needed no instruction to know she was seeing a ghost.

But I don't believe in ghosts, she thought desperately. *I've spent my whole academic career debunking their existence.*

The ghost walked towards Alison, and she saw that it was female – young and beautiful, with short strawberry blonde/brown curls and a good figure beneath her clothes. Her clothes were modern – jeans, T-shirt, and jacket – ruling out the possibility that she was an *old* ghost. Her face was cold, expressionless as a corpse's in its coffin.

Her form faded in and out of view. She never completely disappeared, but never completely solidified either. Alison could see through the woman's face and body to the grass and trees beyond. And all the while that spectral breeze remained, neutralizing the sun's warmth.

"I sense that you don't believe in me," the ghost said.

Alison was frozen with fear, not really sure if her reply would even be audible. "Do I have any choice now?" she whispered in reply.

"My name is Lucy Westerna," the ghost said, her monotone voice dismissing Alison's query as irrelevant. "I'm here to warn you of an immense forthcoming evil."

Cold air blew over Alison with her words, as if the wind was her breath.

"Evil?"

Lucy frowned, her eyes cold and emotionless. She indicated the ruins around them with both hands. "I died here, in this building. I was raped and murdered in *this* very room – on the day the institute burnt down. I died fighting to destroy a monstrous evil – an evil which Jackie Nixon seeks to revive again."

"Jackie Nixon?" Alison was now having trouble thinking. The idea that she was having a conversation with a ghost – disbeliever that she was – unnerved her, threatening to make her flee screaming across the field.

The ghost sensed her fear. "Do not be afraid," Lucy reassured her. "I'm not here to hurt you."

"I don't understand," Alison said. "There are many of us here, why tell *me?*"

Lucy's transparent face flickered in a mirthless smile. "Your husband is rebuilding Melas, Alison. That is as well as may be – on its own, Melas is harmless. You must however convince him not to rebuild the Madison House."

"The Madison House? But–"

"If he rebuilds the Madison House, he will set unimaginable horror in motion." She frowned at Alison, stretching out a fading hand to her. "Come, let us walk together through these old grounds. I want to tell you the story of what really happened here."

Bemused, trapped between fear and faith, Alison followed the ghost through the rubble and out onto the grass beyond.

CHAPTER 6

Don Smith smiled. "That was incredible," he said. "Let's do it again."

Jackie Nixon grinned back, then shook her head sadly. "Can't. George and I are driving into Charleston to meet Tyrone and Betsy for an early diner."

She ran delicate fingers over her bared white breasts, and grinned at Don's hangdog expression. "How about tomorrow, say four in the afternoon? George is seeing Doctor Jones then."

Don nodded; that would have to do. He wasn't completely satisfied, but his lust would keep. Jackie got out of bed. They were in one of the newly rebuilt apartments at the Townhouse Motor Lodge, which Jackie had had renovated for guests.

She and her husband lived a short ten minutes' drive away in The Waldomore Mansion, a neoclassic Greek building that the couple had acquired in downtown Clarksburg so that they could be close to the action over in Melas.

Don and Alison had moved from their residence north of Morgantown to the construction camp in Melas, eighty miles away. Rather than going to his place or Jackie's mansion, Don met her at the Townhouse, ostensibly to discuss business, the motor lodge being much closer to the camp than his place and less conspicuous than hers, for obvious reasons.

Don sat up and watched Jackie get dressed.

Wow, he thought, surveying her perfect figure. *That's what seventeen billion dollars gets you. Oh, fucking yes.*

A momentary comparison with Alison jumped into Don's mind. He quickly dismissed it as an unfair comparison: *Alison hasn't got billions of dollars. If she had, she'd look flawless too. All excessively rich women look perfect.*

Jackie's body wasn't just perfect; she moved like she knew it was. Her abundance of curves blended into sinuous serpentine motions. It seemed to Don that she was aware of every muscle she possessed, and moved her body to make the maximum impact on him.

And yes, she had definitely made an impact on Don. From her first crooked smile and that barest flick of her eyelashes when she'd met Don and Mike for a final consultation before employing them – to here and fucking now.

***

Moran-Smith wasn't the biggest contracting firm in West Virginia, but they had designed a few things, most notably the new football stadium in Morgantown. Mike Moran believed they'd been awarded the Melas contract simply because Jackie Nixon had the hots for Don.

"Dude, I don't care what she wants in bed. Whatever she says – you do," Mike had insisted when

Don informed him that they were sleeping together. "Even if she wants you to pee on each other while eating roasted toads together."

Don had laughed.

Mike tried to look serious. "Dude, just don't screw this up for us – screw Mrs. Nixon instead." He made a pumping gesture with his fist, "Remember, as long as Jackie gets laid – we're made."

Don rolled his eyes: "Why don't *you* seduce her?"

Mike laughed. "Me? Who'd want me?" He wrinkled his brow, "Okay, except my super-fertile redhead at home."

Don had laughed at that. Mike was tall and thin with a bald spot and a potbelly. His glasses made his brown eyes look larger than they were. In addition, Mike was supremely boring. His only interests were his job and his constantly increasing family. An absolute genius with a slide rule, Microsoft Visio and AutoCAD, the life of the party Mike Moran was not. Don had often wondered why Hilary – who was undeniably super-hot even at forty-two – had married and stuck with his best friend all these years. He had a sneaking suspicion that it was because Hilly didn't like sex much and wanted to be with someone like Mike who she could manipulate into only sleeping with her when she wanted to – or when she wanted a kid.

Unlike Alison, though, Hilly liked kids. To Don, that counted for something. She and Mike had seven now, and Hilly had hinted that they planned on trying for 'one or two more' before menopause switched her ovaries off.

66

***

Don turned his mind from the reasons. Mike was right about his relationship with Jackie Nixon and whatever happened, he wasn't messing it up.

Not that he wanted to. Jackie wasn't hard to satisfy. She liked her sex simple, without frills – which amused Don, since even Alison had her kinky days. But Jackie? No. She liked it direct: sometimes hard, sometimes soft, but either way, just basic lovemaking.

Don smiled at the sight of Jackie's backside, bisected into eggs by the strap of her thong. *That's quite an ass,* he thought. She clearly had a sun-lamp regimen, since she was perfectly tanned – no bikini lines at all. Jackie wriggled into her red leather skirt, shaking her ass at Don as she zipped up. Don saw her staring at him, and contrived to look as sad as he could.

Jackie laughed, "No point looking so upset, I'm not giving you head again today, no matter how hard you beg. Get dressed and let's go. George'll soon start calling me."

Don got out of bed and pulled on his trousers. He had met George Nixon on several occasions, and liked him. The billionaire was a pleasant old man; shriveled in his wheelchair, his burning, fervent eyes the only alive part of him. But Don found it impossible to imagine old George Nixon – who looked like he had one foot in the grave – in bed with the effervescent, vivacious Jackie. This was the main reason he didn't feel bad about sleeping with George's wife.

Jackie Nixon checked her watch. She had an hour and a half before meeting up with George so they could go and see Tyrone and Betty. Like Don, she wasn't fully satisfied with their lovemaking, but she needed to discuss something with him: the critical next phase of her plan. She combed her hair, did her lipstick, and then turned to face Don. He was just pulling on his jacket. Jackie smiled her approval of her lover. She'd chosen well. Before selecting the firm to design her new town, Jackie Nixon had done extensive homework.

Private detectives had collected information on all the applicants and Jackie had settled on Donovan Smith because in addition to him being cute and handsome, his wife Alison wasn't the hottest woman in town. Most of the other architects and engineers had trophy wives, in some cases even better looking that Jackie herself. That was a no-no. Even the insipid Mike Moran – whom her investigators had assured her was the smarter of the two Moran-Smith partners – had a beauty queen at home. All were married to knockouts, except for Don Smith, whose missus looked like she'd been conceived in a library. Jackie had smiled at her first sight of the couple.

Yes, Don, she'd thought. *You definitely look like you could use something more exciting in bed.*

She discovered she was right. Don scratched her itch properly. As Don had surmised, George simply wasn't up to it anymore. His equipment worked fine, but his doctors were so scared that he'd have a heart attack that they'd practically begged Jackie to screw someone else. Jackie had obliged, initially not willingly – but what else was she to do? Vibrators definitely weren't her thing.

But . . . her selection of Don Smith had to do with more than just sex. Much, much more. She needed a man she could control. Along with her research into his home life, Jackie Nixon had also requested a psychological profile of Donovan Smith. The results showed he was perfect for what she wanted done. Donovan Smith had been fighting uphill all his professional life, and in contract after contract, Moran-Smith had endlessly been trumped by larger companies. Don's mental profile stated clearly that he wasn't about letting *anything* stand in the way of his chance to enter the big time. *Nothing.* Not even some rather unusual requests. Like the one Jackie had for him now.

Jackie smiled at Don, "Darling, I need you to do something for me."

She delighted in his puppy dog smile. "Anything, Jackie, just ask."

She lowered her voice conspiratorially, "The problem is that we need to keep this just between ourselves."

Don nodded, "I don't see a problem with that."

Jackie smiled coolly, "You soon will."

Now Don looked worried. "This isn't illegal, is it? You're not thinking up some tax evasion scam?"

Jackie's eyes narrowed. She decided this was a good time to find out how far her psychological control over Don went. She'd been assured it was complete. *Okay, now let's see how complete.*

She scowled, her eyes thinning to hostile slits, "Don't you ever dare suggest I'm a fraud again, Donovan, or we're fucking through. I've worked my ass off for everything—"

"I'm sorry," he quickly interjected, his expression VERY worried.

"Just don't do it again," Jackie snapped.

"I said I'm sorry. Tax evasion is about the only crime you super-rich ever get arraigned for."

Jackie pretended to calm down. Secretly, she was immensely pleased. "Okay, sweetie, so you didn't mean it. Now listen to me. What I want you to do isn't illegal. It can, however, be very misconstrued, if the public gets to hear of it."

Don heaved an audible sigh of relief. "It involves the construction then?"

She smiled, "Yes and no. Not the overall project. I need someone I can trust..." She ran her toes up the inside of his left trouser leg for emphasis, "...to oversee a private renovation project for me. I want to rebuild an old house for my husband and myself to live in at the new town."

Don was incredulous. "That's all? That's what you want kept secret?" His face scrunched up in thought. "I don't see what the big deal is. Mike and I are going to have our hands incredibly full for the next nine months at least rebuilding the town..."

"Forget the damn town! This is much more important!"

Don looked into her eyes. She was serious. "All I was about to say," he enunciated slowly, "is that you're saying this is an old house you want rebuilt, so the plans must be in the state records somewhere. With those available, any architect – even a mere draughtsman – can handle the rebuilding."

"You're missing the point, darling," Jackie said. "I need someone I can trust."

"To build a *house?* C'mon, Jackie honey, be reasonable."

She smiled sweetly, "Oh, but this isn't any normal house. It's the old Madison House up on Raccoon Run Road; it's a historical site."

"So what's so secretive about it?"

"Well, for one thing, to commemorate all the dead in that terrible flood, I want it rebuilt using the sediment at the bottom of the Floyd Lake crater as the construction sand in the mortar."

Don just stared at her. Her request made no sense whatsoever to him.

Jackie smiled at his confusion. "But first things first, darling, I need to know – can it be done? Not the actual construction; but will the crater soil hold together well enough? I don't want a house that'll crumble on me."

Don considered the puzzle. "Most lake sediments in this region are clay. If you bake clay the proper way, you can make bricks or perhaps decorative stones with it. So, in short answer, it can," he said finally. "We'll analyze the sediment to see its composition to determine how to mix the cement."

Jackie heaved a sigh of relief, "I'm so glad that won't be a problem."

Her phone rang. She picked it up. "Yes, George, darling, I'll be with you in fifteen minutes. I'm just leaving my meeting with Mr. Smith."

She smiled at Don. "Marital duty calls."

Don nodded. Then the warm afternoon sun filtering in through the drapes somehow suddenly turned cold on Don's skin. He had the chilling sensation that there was something very wrong about Jackie's intent to use the Floyd Lake sediment as building material. He felt the wrongness deep inside him, but he just had no idea what it was; no explanation to his weird feeling.

They made their way downstairs, and before entering their separate cars, Jackie hugged Don tight.

"Remember our date tomorrow," she whispered throatily in his ear. They separated, and she patted her ass. "I'm keeping this warm for you till then."

Don smiled. For the first time since he'd begun sleeping with Jackie Nixon, he was glad to be separated from her. He decided to go home. Alison would be out for sure, which was great. Don was spooked. He needed to think.

Driving away from their tryst, Don's reservations faded. Soon, he was uncertain what he'd been so worried about. A mere chill in the air and he was scared!

Thousands died in this town, he thought, *many of those when the lake ruptured. So what? What better way can there be to celebrate those whose lives had been cut so tragically short than to...*

Enough of this! he decided firmly. *Jackie wants a fucking house, I'll build it for her. I'll do fucking anything for her – fucking anything.*

The obsessiveness of this last thought was totally lost on him. Feeling much better all of a sudden, Don changed his mind about going home. He spun his car around and headed off for work.

His thoughts shifted from Jackie's odd request to the woman herself. Jackie wasn't better in bed than Alison – far from it. The IDEA of Jackie Nixon, however, the sheer polished glamour of her, *was* better than Alison's mousy dowdiness.

Heading over to join Mike and the rest of their team, Donovan Smith harbored no illusions whatsoever that this was anything more than a passing affair, or that he was more than stress relief to Jackie Nixon. He hated himself for cheating on Alison – but only a little. As long as Alison never found out about the affair, Don saw no threat to their marriage. He was certain that this fling of theirs would end when the construction of Melas did, and then he'd likely never see Jackie Nixon again.

CHAPTER 7

Alison stood outside Walter Pinkman's house. Lucy Westerna, the ghost at the construction camp site, had directed her here.

"Root amongst the papers in his study. You'll find much to interest you," the ghost had said.

Alison, still reeling from her acknowledgment of the ghost's existence had jumped into her car and headed over there. Google Maps was fantastic; even through the devastation of Raccoon Run Road, she was able to locate the Pinkman house.

The house itself was an old, two-story 1940s-era mock-Victorian, sided with salmon-colored asbestos shingles. For its age, it looked in fairly decent shape from the outside, being one of the few structures left standing in Melas. This might have been due to the fact that it resided halfway up a long, winding hill that ended in the spot where the Madison House once stood. Being on the hill, even partway up, it was spared from the full blast of the flood that took out most of the town when Talman Cain blew up the dam at Floyd Lake.

Of particular curiosity to Alison was a large amount of burnt rocks strung out all over the yard. The rocks did not appear to be of the limestone or sandstone native to the region, but were of marble appearance, and looked as if a large explosion had occurred near the drive way to the house and the rock fragments were the result. Alison wondered what had caused this debris field and guessed that maybe the flood had brought it into the yard. She felt a chill run down her spine as she carefully navigated her way through the rubble and over to the porch. Taking a deep breath, Alison pushed the door of the old house open and peered inside.

The interior was dark and musty. Alison had expected this. The cream wallpaper was muddy and bloated, the carpeting rotted – all evidence of the flooding, at least on the first floor. Watching out for rats, she made her way upstairs.

Walter Pinkman's study was a window-filled, upstairs room with a view of the Floyd Lake crater. The floodwaters evidently hadn't risen this high. Other than a thin layer of dust over everything, the room was still in good condition. The early afternoon sun shining into the room lit it well, to the point where Alison could see newly-disturbed dust particles floating about in the sun's rays.

On entering the study, Alison's attention was instantly captured by the excessive amount of arcane paraphernalia on display. Around the room, on shelves and the desk, were various chalices, ankhs, and one by one, Alison noticed there were three human skulls in the room, one set in a white plate stained with what had to be blood.

There were also several tall shelves of books. Most were black leather-bound journals that were nondescript from a distance, and could have been mistaken for a collection of old encyclopedias. Alison pulled one from the shelf and flipped through it. *Scriptures of Qabbalists* was inscribed on the first page, followed by a text in a foreign language that Alison could not interpret. She pulled another that was in English that described the ceremonial worship of the Ancient Egyptians and contained many hand-drawn obelisks and arcane symbols that Alison assumed were hieroglyphics. A third notebook simply inscribed with the letters *BAPHOMET* had images of a winged, bat-like creature with a goat's head. There were many different drawings of the bat and under each, certain Latin phrases that Alison could not interpret. Oddly, however, there was one drawing of a bat with a human head with the word "Legion" under it. Another page was marked "Incantation Rites / Modus Operandi." A fourth book was called *Ensnaring the Spirits,* which contained rituals on how to intercept the soul of a newly deceased person and trap it in a stone, thereby preventing it from going to heaven or hell. It contained copious notes on how to use the life force within the stones to serve the will of the possessor of the stone.

This is a sorcerer's treasure trove in here! Alison thought, a chill penetrating her breast. *This man was definitely a student of the dark arts.*

Before entering his study, Alison had had doubts over Lucy Westerna's claim that Walter Pinkman had been a necromancer. Now she had none.

Above an inverted cross hung left of the window, was a framed photograph. It depicted Pinkman smiling whilst carrying a little girl of about six, a pretty blonde child with an impish smile. The picture was faded and had to be quite old. Alison found the picture's bright happiness incongruous with the darkness the rest of the room projected. A feeling of unease settled on Alison as she looked around the study from object to object. The displayed relics conveyed an ethereal atmosphere simply by being here. Her chill returned.

Then she grinned. *I came to Melas to find evidence of superstition. I've sure hit the mother lode quickly.*

Then, remembering what the ghost had told her, Alison tempered her excitement. Dusting off the begrimed chair, she sat at Walter Pinkman's study table, pulled a pile of his papers and books towards her and began reading through them. She skimmed through most, looking for information about the old Madison mansion and what it represented. Alison soon found what she was looking for. It was a small diary. She began reading it. The more Alison read the more alarmed she became. Soon she was very worried.

Vampirism? Who would ever believe such a thing was possible?

***

That night at dinner both Donovan and Alison Smith were rather silent. Neither marital partner noticed that the other was similarly unwilling to speak, since they were too submerged in their own thoughts. Their minds were both occupied with Jackie Nixon.

Don was preoccupied with working out how to build the Madison House. There was no conceivable way of doing it without Mike finding out, so he'd told his partner.

The pair had been standing under a tree rechecking the university plans. A short distance off, a subcontracted engineering team from Charleston was at work taking measurements.

Mike had listened to Donovan explain Jackie's request, then smiled. "Sure, if that's what she wants," he said, his tone blasé.

"She wants it kept silent."

Mike had shrugged, taken off his glasses, misted them with his breath, and replaced them. "So? She's rich enough to be eccentric," he'd smiled. "You should be grateful she doesn't want you to fill the lake with sharks or crocodiles and you to go swimming in the nude there."

Donovan was worried. "You don't care?"

Mike shook his head. He peered at Don, a smug grin plastered on his face, "What's to worry about? That your super-rich girlfriend wants to secretly rebuild an old mansion? You're not superstitious are you?"

Don had felt a slight return of the previous chill. He'd laughed it off. "Superstitious? Dude, that's Alison's department."

Mike laughed too. Then he became serious, "Way I see this, it's simply more leverage for us." He wagged a finger at Don, "Don't get me wrong – not to blackmail Jackie, but if you're building her dream house for her, under whatever crackpot schematics she has in mind, it solidifies her trust in us." He'd winked, "May even lead to new contracts after this one."

So now, at dinner, Don was occupied with working out how to keep 'the project' out of the public eye. Not that there was any public there. But there was always the possibility of the builders talking to the wrong people.

Don finally resolved his issue. The solution was simple. He'd use different teams. First, a spurious 'geological survey' team from out of state would collect the lake sediment and deliver it to the construction site. Then, once enough had been collected to build the house, the 'geologists' would be dismissed, and the actual builders hired – also from out of West Virginia.

Alison spooned chicken and noodles into her mouth, chewing and swallowing it mechanically. She was unaware of the food's taste, although she was a halfway decent cook when it came to whipping up dinner.

She tried to think up a sensible way to tell and convince Don *not* to construct the Madison house. The 'You know, honey, a ghost told me this morning...' approach was definitely off the cards; especially for her – the professional skeptic. Alison's problem seemed a massive one. According to Lucy Westerna, Jackie Nixon had made her request to Don this morning, and Don had accepted supervising the construction of the Madison residence. It complicated matters that Don hadn't mentioned Jackie's request to

Alison. That clearly meant he didn't think Jackie's request either odd or important. He was here to build, after all. One more house made no difference.

Alison looked across to her husband, his brow furrowed in thought as he spooned Lo Mein into his mouth. He caught her gazing at him and smiled, "Tastes wonderful, darling."

Alison smiled back. Both partners returned their minds to their thoughts.

Though now convinced beyond a doubt of the truth of the ghost's words, Alison realized she had to wait till Don said something about the Madison house first. He was sure to do so once he got rid of whatever he had on his mind now.

And if Don said nothing, she'd prompt the conversation.

PART 2

THE VAMPIRE FARM

CHAPTER 8

SIX MONTHS LATER

"I am not a naturally superstitious man," Martin Tarrant said. "I was a Major in Uncle Sam's Army, peace keeping in the gulf – the most down-to-earth guy you could meet. But circumstances, however, compel me to believe in life after death."

He smiled, which – in William's opinion – was little different from his frown.

"And other, even stranger things." He looked at William and Kate in turn. "I'd like to make a proposition to you both."

"Please go on," Kate said. "What brings you here to us?"

William nodded, but said nothing. He was bothered by Tarrant's sudden arrival on their doorstep. Martin Tarrant was middle-aged. He was tall and rugged, with a weather-worn face and cold gray eyes. William had immediately noted the man's military bearing, of which Kate seemed oblivious. To him, Tarrant looked like a killer – ruthless, cold, efficient. Whatever Tarrant wanted with them both couldn't be good. William already suspected that it was bad. Very bad.

Martin Tarrant nodded. "First, permit me to explain how I found you, William."

"I'm more interested in *why* you're here," William said. He was becoming edgy. His sense of misgiving refused to leave him.

Martin Tarrant smiled again. "I have a peculiar problem," he said. "One I think you can help me with. I need your help to trap a vampire."

William froze. Beside him, Kate drew in breath in a sharp gasp and gripped his hand tightly.

"A vampire?" Kate said. "Surely you don't believe in things like that?"

William didn't trust himself to speak.

Tarrant frowned. "I have no choice but to believe," he said in a sad voice. "My elder brother, Joe, was killed by one." His expression became more morose, "My brother was a trucker. A year ago, he delivered a large drill to crews responding to the accident at the Dark Hollows coal mine. He was there on the night the flood hit the town."

William now found his voice, "So why do you think a vampire killed him? The flood killed just about everyone in the town that night."

"Not everyone," Tarrant said emphatically. "My brother got out alive, but he was later found dead in his truck just north of Marietta, Ohio. Joe had two large punctures in his neck and all the blood had been drained from his body. No one could make anything of it."

Kate squeezed William's hand tighter. Her nervousness transmitted itself to him.

"All I had to go on," Tarrant continued, "was that Joe called me from his cell the night he died. He was in a truck stop bathroom and mentioned he'd picked up a hitchhiker who he recognized as an old high school buddy of his – Jeff Abraham – but weirdly, he'd told Joe, 'You can call me Victor.'" William's eyebrows shot up at the name, and Tarrant continued, grimly.

"Joe remembered his buddy's fate from the news – he was the miner who had escaped the coal mine collapse only to die once he made it out. Joe wondered if he was transporting a ghost. I laughed it off; he seemed better for my bullshit, and we hung up.

"That's the last I heard from him. Shortly after, Joe was found dead at the truck stop. I came over for Jack's burial. Once I saw those punctures on his throat..." He fell silent, his cold face wracked by emotion.

"I don't believe in vampires," William said.

Tarrant laughed mirthlessly. "Father Demetrius at the seminary says different," Tarrant replied, his voice cold. "He said you believe a lot of things, but those are beside the point." He smirked at the surprise in William's face. "I was going to explain how I came to know about you. Father Demetrius is my youngest brother. He told me everything – what you claim happened to you at Melas. And how you quit the seminary because they didn't believe you." He looked searchingly at William. "I find it odd, you know. That with everything that happened to you, you could walk away from the ministry that easily."

"I... I..." Again, William had no words. No defense. He looked helplessly at Kate, who came to his rescue.

"He just got worked up," she said. "We all make mistakes."

Tarrant laughed, looking appreciatively at Kate, "Yes we do; and sometimes mistakes get us very pretty rewards."

Kate smiled in acknowledgement of the compliment, "But still, how can we – I mean William – help you?"

Tarrant's humor wiped off his face. "It's simple: I want to find and kill the vampire who murdered my brother. I'm a military man. War has been my life for the past thirty-five years. I've been in situations you wouldn't believe on behalf of this country. Afghanistan, Iraq, Columbia, Sudan – you name the country Uncle Sam had a beef with, I've fought there. But that's natural warfare. What I'm about taking on here is a supernatural opponent – something I've never faced before." He looked pointedly at William. "You, William, however, have faced and beaten vampires – not once, but twice. I'd like to recruit you to help me take out mine."

"I'm not interested," William said. "I'm burnt out."

Tarrant nodded, "I expected you to say that. My brother says you barely escaped with your life…"

William found a smile. "I didn't escape," he said wearily. "I was killed and went to hell, from where Jesus resurrected me."

Tarrant nodded again, "I'll offer you a million dollars for your assistance. Up front. Just name your bank."

William looked Tarrant cold in the eyes. "No. You can't buy me."

Kate turned to look at William, "Darling, we can use the money. I think we should at least consider his request. A million dollars…"

William shook his head, "You've no idea what we'd be getting into. I do, and my answer's no."

Kate's gaze hardened. William ignored how pissed-off with him she looked. *This is all for the best. She has no idea,* he thought.

"I'm sorry, Mr. Tarrant," he began, "but…"

Now Tarrant smiled for real, "If you're this principled, you'd have made a great priest," he said smoothly.

William winced. The statement was all the more painful because Tarrant seemed sincere. "I'm sorry I can't help you, Martin," he said. "I really don't want to ask you to leave, but it's been a hectic day and…"

"The vampire I'm after is Victor Rothenstein," Tarrant said.

William froze. "Victor? It can't be – we killed him."

Tarrant smiled now he saw he had William's attention. "Not completely. Apparently, he can switch his soul between host bodies. I have made some investigations, and discovered some very interesting things. Now he's residing in a man called Jeff Abraham."

He frowned, "There's another detail you need to know. Your baby cousin – the Harkers' son – isn't dead. He was kidnapped."

William felt like he'd been smashed over the head with a hammer. He shook his head violently from side to side. "What the fuck!" William managed to exclaim. "That can't be true. I was there at the hospital on the night they died – hell, I was at the funeral home and made a speech! What you are saying just cannot be real."

"Well, let me asked you this," Terrant spoke in a soft voice, "Did you actually see the three bodies?"

A moment passed and William mumbled, "Only Jon's. The others were too badly burned, the doctor advised me not to see them."

"And the funeral," Terrant pressed, "was it closed casket?"

William nodded.

"Then it is possible. Victor Rothenstein both masterminded the Harkers' deaths and kidnapped their newborn child."

"Why would he do something like that?" Kate asked, horrified.

"Possibly to turn the child into a vampire," Tarrant said. "It would be the utmost revenge for what you cost him, wouldn't it?"

William nodded. His heart suddenly felt like a hole in his chest, filled with despair. "I'll help you hunt Victor," he said quietly.

"One million dollars, right?" Kate prompted.

Tarrant nodded. He smiled coldly at Kate, his battle-weathered face creasing up like he was scrutinizing an enemy captive. "Just give me an account number."

"What do we do now?" William asked.

"You wait till I contact you again," Tarrant replied.

"That's it? Just wait?"

Smiling thinly, Tarrant nodded. "I share your impatience, but waiting isn't my first choice either. My people – I've assembled a team – are trying to locate Victor – Jeff Abrahams' – actual location. We found him initially by tracking withdrawals from Rothenstein's old accounts even after he was believed dead. Using this technique, we've narrowed his whereabouts to somewhere in northeast Ohio. But we're still trying to find his actual hideout."

Tarrant pulled out a clip of money from his jacket. He passed this to Kate, along with a business card, "Here's twenty grand for expenses. Buy whatever you think we'll need to take down the vampire." Tarrant got to his feet. "Now I must be going; I'm late for an appointment." He nodded to them both. "Call the number on the card or use the email to send me your banking details."

Kate nodded, "We'll do that."

"We don't need Tarrant's money," William said once he'd left.

Kate wrinkled her nose at him. "Don't we? With a million dollars, we can get married. I can stop busting my ass as a K-Mart cashier and you can stop working in that machine shop. We could start our own business… raise our own family."

"That's true," William began cautiously. She was, of course, right. "It's just that, taking Tarrant's money…"

"…taints the purity of your revenge, and makes you nothing more than a bounty hunter in your eyes," Kate finished for him. She leaned forward, stared intently at him, her blue eyes boring into his.

"Yes, exactly," William agreed. "My cousin is also involved in this. It seems wrong to profit from his danger."

Kate laughed, "From what Tarrant says, young master Harker might be part of the danger." She saw how her comment pained William, and stopped laughing, "I apologize for that, darling – you're right; it isn't funny in the least. But I understand your reasoning. You've a natural altruism in your makeup." She smiled, "You're wonderful, darling, but America doesn't care that you've saved it from the end of the world. We need money; the more of it we have, the better. No point refusing Tarrant's cash. What I suggest is that we take out this vampire and once we've done that, we'll…"

"Why do you keep saying *we?* You're staying *here*, well out of harm's way." He winced, seeing the look on her face.

"I'm coming," Kate said. "I want to see what a vampire looks like."

William sighed, "Kate, this isn't a joyride. I could die for real out there. No I forgot – I already did, once! Only thing is, this time there won't be any Jay Christiano around to resurrect me." He gazed fondly at Kate, "I've no idea how powerful Victor is now, or what other powers he's developed. I was shocked to hear he can switch bodies – that's new. No, darling. You stay where it's nice and safe."

"Oh no, I won't," Kate said. "I'm coming too. All you tough, alpha-male, macho vampire killers are going to need my help."

Now William was amused, "Oh, yeah? Educate me – in what way do Tarrant and his crew need the help a 120 pound weakling like you to catch a vampire?"

Kate smiled sweetly, "The baby, darling. How many of you guys have any idea how to change a dirty diaper?"

Her argument stumped William. Caring for the rescued Harker baby was the one thing Tarrant wouldn't be thinking of; he was interested in revenge. Still…

"But Kate," William said gently, reaching out and stroking her blonde hair, looking into her beautiful blue eyes, "Kate, darling, you know nothing about vampires. Nothing at all. This…"

She silenced him with a finger across his lips, then bent and kissed him. Despite his misgivings, and his clear sense that she'd just manipulated him to achieve her own purpose, William kissed her back passionately. He loved her so much.

Kate raised her lips from Williams and smiled at him, her blue eyes once again boring into his. "You're right, darling," she said. "I know next to nothing about vampires. But you know a lot, and I think it's time you taught me."

William thought about it. He nodded, "Okay, since you insist on coming along…"

"Oh, I fucking do insist, darling."

"Well then, the main thing to remember when dealing with vampires – is never to let them bite you. If they do, you'll become like them."

Kate looked at William aghast. "That's *all?* Dude, even kids in kindergarten know that."

William looked at her poker-faced. Then burst into laughter, "There are other things, but I thought it best to start you off simple."

A giggling Kate leapt on him and began pummeling him with her fists. "Oh, don't you ever make fun of me like that, Mr. McConnellson. I mean ever again, or I'll kill you!"

Busy having their mock fight, and soon after, kissing passionately, neither Kate nor William noticed the muted news update that screened on their ignored TV, about Jackie Nixon, entitled: 'Construction of New Melas Now Well Underway.'

CHAPTER 9

Nightfall.

The black Lexus RX350 sped down Interstate 80 toward Warren, Ohio. Its drivers were two women in their mid-twenties, both attractive. The driver, Laura, was a blonde; the other, Judy, a brunette. Both women were impeccably turned out, their clothes and makeup perfect, as if they were about to attend a party or movie premiere.

Both women also had pallid complexions and blood red eyes. Laura handled the Lexus with calm confidence. She looked over at Judy and frowned.

"No one so far," she said angrily. "I don't fancy pork juice again tonight."

Judy nodded, "Me neither. Cathy don't seem to care, though."

Laura smirked, "She's infatuated with Victor and his 'Master Plan,' that's all. Mother of a new race and the other bullshit."

"Not bullshit," Judy cautioned, her voice wary and low, as if Victor could hear them, even out here. "You know as well as I do that soon..."

Laura calmed down, "You're right: *soon*. But right now, I feel a like a heroin addict having to make do with methadone when there's a veritable river of pure junk flowing around me.   Every time I see someone I feel like leaping…"

"Sssshhh!" Judy said, tapping Laura's gear-shift hand. "Up ahead!"

Laura looked. She smiled on seeing the solitary figure illuminated in the headlights near the edge of the road, and stated, "Seems our luck's in."

The hitchhiker was a man in his mid-thirties, with dark hair and eyes, and a trimmed mustache. He was dressed in faded denim and boots. He picked up his pack when the Lexus pulled up by him, his smile as he peered in the window tinged with relief.

"Which way you headed?" Judy asked.

"Warren." He had the barest of Latino accents.

Laura deactivated the lock on the rear door, saying, "Get in, we're headed that way ourselves."

He got in and shut the door. "My name's Jose," he said. "Thanks for stopping. Been trying to hitch a ride for four hours, now. I'd begun thinking I'd have to sleep out in the wild tonight."

Judy turned back to smile at him, "You're welcome. I'm Judy and this is Laura. You new to these parts?"

He nodded, "I'm from Illinois; been traveling east, looking for work."

Judy flashed Laura a predatory look, which Jose, seated in the SUV's rear shadows, didn't notice. Laura laughed.

"You any good at farm work?"

Jose nodded, "Last place I worked was on a corn farm in Walkerton, Indiana, but harvest's over now, and the work's slow. Time to move on." He laughed, "But why the questions? You women don't look like farmers."

"Our uncle is," Laura said. She parked the car, and looked back at Jose. *He's quite handsome*, she thought, an older instinctive hunger replacing her bloodlust.

"Judy's telling the truth," she told Jose. "Our uncle Victor farms pigs. He's always looking for help; in fact he mentioned something about needing someone to operate some new piece of equipment two days ago." She looked at Judy. "What was that god-fangled contraption called again?"

Judy shrugged back at her, "An MG-800 grinder something or other. Something for making sausages."

"A meat grinder," Jose said. "That sounds like quite a big operation."

"Not really. But he does supply a good number of restaurants and organic markets in Warren. You know, this is Amish country, so people like the freshest meats and produce." She smiled at Jose, "So what you say? You interested in the job? The turn-off to the farm's a mile ahead."

Jose smiled, "Sure thing! Let's go."

Laura grinned, "Not yet, darling." She winked at Judy, "There's something you can do for us first." She unbuttoned her top. Jose's eyes widened as she freed her breasts.

Judy giggled. She slid down her panties and kicked them off, making sure Jose could see what she'd done, drawling, "Pig farming's a hard job, Jose.

We need to first make certain you're up to the task before recommending you to Old Uncle Victor."

Jose nodded. Sweat began beading on his forehead. "Sure . . . Yes, of course . . ."

"Good. Let's find somewhere less... public, then." Laura started the car up and turned down a lane to a secluded spot, pulled the car over and climbed into the rear of the Lexus.

Jose began unbuttoning his pants. His erection sprang out like a jack-in-the-box that had been too tightly wound. He never noticed the red glow of Laura's eyes as she enveloped his member in her mouth, wrapping her blood-red lips around the engorged shaft.

Jose gasped and maneuvered into a more comfortable position, pushing his pants down below his knees.

Then Judy joined her sister for a three-way romp in the back seat.

CHAPTER 10

Seated in his study, staring at the clock on the wall, Victor took a sip from his cup of swine blood. He was a tall man of muscular build now with the physical body of Jeff Abraham, but with the Romanian accent of his possessor, Victor Rothenstein. Victor was now adjusting to life as someone else. He'd been surprised to find himself in Jeff Abraham's body.

The real-life Jeff Abraham had been a coal miner after a stint in prison, falsely convicted of murdering his wife a few years before. In ironic coincidence, it had been the real Victor Rothenstein who had taken Jeff's wife, Lillian Abraham, to be a vampire mistress. Although she had died, it was not at her husband's hand, as authorities had originally suspected.

Fleeing the meltdown and flooding in Melas, he'd gotten a lift from a trucker leaving the godforsaken area after a delivery and returning home with his empty rig. The man had been a calm personable fellow, and Victor would have liked to let him live, but the bloodlust had been too strong.

Whilst drinking the trucker's blood, the master had spoken to him. The beast's infernal voice had throbbed like a headache in his skull: "Do not be surprised, my servant. Your renewed life is a reward for a job well done."

"But you're dead, master."

"No more so than you," the master had replied. "The apocalypse will still come, for it is fated to do so. The events in Melas only postponed the inevitable. Certain matters must occur first, before the new end. I will, however, contact you when it is time for us to re-stake our claim to Earth and eternity. But for now, we watch and wait. You must regain your strength, for there are still many threats to the actualization of our intents."

Victor – his lips painted with blood from the trucker's ripped-open throat – had smiled. "I will wait, master. Your will is my desire."

The black presence had faded from Victor's head. It had not returned since.

So now, Victor waited. He waited on his pig farm in the middle of Ohio, sustaining himself primarily on the blood of his herds. He worked on making himself as inconspicuous as possible. It upset Victor greatly that he'd lost all his papers in the destruction of his personal mansion, the Madison House, in Melas. But still, he could rebuild. Most books had copies; it just took time to find them.

Victor was presently quite disgruntled. Laura and Judy should have returned from Cleveland an hour ago, with one of two very rare artifacts – documents – from Doctor Herman Thayer. He would only be getting one of them this evening. Doctor Thayer was having some difficulties persuading the seller to part with the other parchment he was interested in. "I'll have it in a couple days," he had assured. As for tonight's find…

Damn sluts, he thought angrily. *Most likely screwing about again.*

Victor got up and turned on the television. Once again the news was about this woman, Jackie Nixon, who was rebuilding Melas. Victor had an odd feeling each time he looked at Mrs. Nixon. She clearly wasn't a vampire – as she was out in daylight – but there was something 'not right' about her. He smiled. She was beautiful though, a blonde bombshell, the kind of woman a man wanted warming his bed. Sex with her was certain to be a lot of fun.

Idly, Victor wondered if it would be possible to contact Mrs. Nixon; wondered if she'd be susceptible to being converted into a vampire. He toyed with the idea for a while, then dropped it. *No, I must take no chance. I was careless that first time in Melas – a fatal mistake I will not repeat again. Jackie Nixon is too high-profile a celebrity to suddenly disappear without questions being asked. And there are any number of self-styled 'vampire hunters' looking for a heart to stake.*

Victor parted the window drapes to let the moonlight in. He stood by the window and looked out over his farm. The farm occupied a thirty-acre lot south of the town of Warren and well off the travelled thoroughfare, where it wasn't even possible to hear Interstate traffic rumble past. The land was fertile, rolling hill land, with a stream at its northern border. Frankie and Marv, Victor's two hands, had more than once suggested that Victor pasture sheep on it.

"We's make a sure killing, Mr. Victor," Frankie would say, his pockmarked face beaming its idiotic smile. "Sheep's be so happy here, they's shit theyselves for joy!"

Directly opposite the farmhouse, about a hundred yards away, were the three pig enclosures, long wood-walled, aluminum-roofed buildings. A distance from them, connected by a conveyor belt, stood the meat processing plant. Beside this were parked two farm trucks and a delivery van. On their far side stood the quarters for the farm help, a large cottage split into four self-contained apartments.

The farm house itself was a two-story stone building, with a large basement. The basement had been the clincher to Victor's buying this particular farm. A vampire needed a lair – somewhere to sleep during the day, and the basement now held four jeweled coffins: one each for Judy and Laura, Victor and... Cathy.

As if on cue, Cathy entered the study.

"You're not drinking the blood tonight?" Cathy Edwards was a thirty-something small, thin brunette with perky breasts and shoulder-length hair.

Victor turned and frowned. "It's a tiring taste," he replied. "It's irritating with so many humans out there, to be reduced to this." He indicated the cup of pig's blood.

Cathy nodded, walked over to him and gripped his hand in her smaller one. "But remember, you're the one who tells us to be calm; that now isn't the time for action."

Victor looked down at her earnest white face, its eyes as red as his. "True, but... Oh, you're right, of course. It's Judy and Laura who've got me this worked up. Those two sluts should be back by now. That's a very precious document Doctor Thayer..."

"You've called their phones?"

Victor scowled. "Both went direct to voicemail. I should have never listened to you on..."

"Don't get worked up," Cathy said with a smile. "Laura and Judy are both young. They're likely out having fun."

Victor nodded. "As long as I get my document in one piece. Otherwise, I'll–"

"What's so important about this paper?" Cathy said to distract him.

She walked across to his study table, and picked up the cup of blood. Sitting on the table's edge, crossing her legs so her skirt rode up her thighs, she took a sip. The blood was cold now; it had the consistency of yogurt as it went down her throat. Victor turned from the window to face her. His eyes widened slightly in appreciation of Cathy's bloodless thighs.

She smiled at him, "Yes, dear? I'm listening."

"It's not the paper itself that's so important. No, what I mean is, this document is part of a body of knowledge of necromantic rites that I'm working to collect. It might be valueless; it might be essential to our purpose. My main worry is that while partying, our two associates don't *damage* it. Doctor Thayer had been extremely helpful and if..."

Cathy concentrated instead on the pleasure the blood gave her. Refreshing. So, it wasn't human, but beggars couldn't be choosers, and this set-up was so much better than where she'd come from.

Cathy Edwards was also from Melas. She'd fled the town on the same night Victor had, but by a different route. Initially in the grip of an irresistible force pulling her, amongst several hundred other ghouls and vampires, to Floyd Lake, Cathy had fallen into a pit, and had thus missed the inferno that incinerated all who'd walked into the lake. Cathy had finally climbed out of the hole she'd fallen into and hurried to join the others, only to find herself alone on the lake rim, staring down at a pile of smoking ash.

The force compelling Cathy onward had now cut off; making her wonder what she was doing there. She'd turned around and shambled off. For the next six months, she had wandered the West Virginian countryside, sleeping in holes and empty houses in the day, hunting and killing by night.

Six months ago, Frankie and Marv had informed Victor that something was killing his pigs at night. Both men would arrive at work in the morning to find three to four pigs dead. The farm hands – both men of sub-normal intellect, and neither having any idea that their employer was undead – attributed the punctures in the dead animals' necks to snakebite. They had no explanation as to why the corpses were all drained of blood.

Victor, however, knew better. So he'd set a trap, waiting at his window, until he saw the telltale bat shape descend onto the pig enclosure and flitter in through a ventilation grill. Then, his cold heart thrilling joyously at the knowledge that he wasn't alone, he assumed similar form and pursued the interloper.

He'd not been disappointed. The woman he'd startled with her fangs in a pig's neck was attractive, and once she recognized they were both vampires, she was as overjoyed as he was.

They'd drained the dead pig together, then fucked there in the pigswill; a muddy, bloody coupling as if they were pigs themselves. Their passion had been bestial in the extreme. Afterwards they'd killed another three pigs and drunk and bathed in their blood, then had sex again.

The next evening – Victor never held audience with the farm hands before seven p.m. – he introduced Cathy to them as their new mistress.

"Mos' pigs gots killed las' night, boss," Marv said, hitching up his stained overalls. Marv was short, fat and ugly, with a slack jaw confirming his mental deficiency and a horrible mole on his left cheek that had hair in it like a mouse's whiskers. "We'se ground 'em up as sausage meats already and froze 'em, but jus' ter let ya nowse."

"Yes we did, Mr. Victor," Frankie said. Frankie was good-looking, but his eyes had an eternally far-off look in them. "We ground up the dead porkers and stuffed the sausages. You can call McCarthy come pick 'em up tomorraw." He looked cross-eyed at Victor and Cathy. "But, this keeps up, we's soon gon' have too much pork, and people's gon' be suspecting as to why we's killing so many pigs, sir."

"Yes, trues," Marv added. "Too much dead piggers."

"Don't worry, boys," Cathy said with authority. "Rest assured, it won't happen again – we killed the snake last night."

"You'se did?"

"Yes, Marv," Victor said. "You've nothing to be afraid of anymore. Cathy killed it with a spud bar."

Marv, who was deathly afraid of snakes, grinned back. "Thanks, Ms. Cathy."

Grinning broadly, both retarded farm hands left the house.

Now, Cathy finished the cup of pig's blood. Unlike Victor, who looked under immense strain, she felt refreshed, reinvigorated. Cathy felt ready for a long flight out on the wind, black wings beating the night air as she hunted, imagining herself descending on some unsuspecting couple out for a moonlight stroll, sinking her teeth into the man's pale throat while his girlfriend watched, screaming, and drinking, drinking – *Damn, no!* She cut the thoughts off, suddenly as frustrated as Victor. This was the danger. They couldn't just go flying around and killing people. She looked at Victor.

He frowned coldly back at her. "I see you feel it too now. The question is how much longer do we wait? How much longer? The master's will is harsh, with so much food to hand."

Cathy strained against the bloodlust that suddenly squeezed her like a giant hand. Her eyes bulged. Then she sniffed. "I smell blood."

Victor nodded. "I smell it too."

The next moment, the darkness outside the farmhouse was broken by the headlights of Judy and Laura's Lexus SUV.

Cathy smiled at Victor. "I told you I was right about the girls. It looks like we'll dine on prime livestock tonight, my darling."

Victor smiled back, his eyes gleaming in bloodlust.

CHAPTER 11

Laura and Judy staggered into the farmhouse, dragging Jose after them. The trio were grinning, and Jose was still in shock, disbelieving his luck. Both females had been more like animals than women when they'd fucked in the Lexus. Jose's balls felt emptier than they ever had in his life. He was drained.

"Don't tell us you're tired," Laura had teased him afterwards. "There's a lot more to come tonight; just wait till you meet Cathy."

A lot more? And I've not even yet begun working here, Jose thought. *If they keep me screwing like this, I'll never get anything done.*

Laura and Judy steered him through the vestibule, into the dining room. Jose paused before a huge upright freezer.

"What's this for?" he asked in surprise.

Laura laughed, flinging her blonde hair around. "Spare pork."

"Huh?"

Judy nodded. "Uncle Victor ordered one too many freezers for the meat processing plant. It ended up here."

"And occasionally," Laura added, "there's a sausage spillover – too much pork, so they use this one."

106

Jose shrugged, staring at the massive freezer. "Damn," he said, "It's large enough to store someone in. Without chopping them up, even."

Both girls giggled. "Like this is some horror story! C'mon, Jose, let's go meet Uncle Victor."

Victor smiled when the girls led Jose into the dining room. *He looks nice and healthy.*

Turning Judy and Laura had been Cathy's idea. Three months ago, the pair – who were actually sisters, Laura being the older – had walked out of the woods near the farm late one evening. They'd explained that they'd been backpacking across the countryside and decided to take a shortcut through the woods. They had been relying on their cell phones' GPS to guide them, but once their batteries died, they had gotten lost. Showing up at the farmhouse door, they asked if they could please make a call home.

Cathy had invited them in. Victor had wanted to kill Judy and Laura, but Cathy suggested that they turn them instead.

"I disagree," Victor had said. "The danger of our being discovered increases as our number does. The more we are, the more likely one of us slips up, and then…"

"You worry too much," Cathy said in a hoarse whisper. "I intend employing them as hunters. The woods and roads around here are always full of hitchhikers: warm, blood-packed bodies just waiting for us to drain them dry. Kids, vagrants and others no one will miss."

Victor had stared at her brooding, unconvinced.

"Just smell them," Cathy had impressed on him. "Smell the blood pulsing under their skin. Don't lie to me that you don't miss sucking such purity."

To drive her point home, she pushed open the door of the living room.

Inside it, Laura was on the phone. "Yes mom, we're fine, we've turned up at this farm in the middle of nowhere. The nice farmer says they'll give us a ride to town in the morning where we'll catch a bus back to Saginaw…"

Cathy sniffed. "Just smell that hot blood. Tell me you don't want to rip her throat open and drain her dry right now."

"I still don't like it," Victor said stubbornly. "What do we need them for? We can pick up the hitchhikers ourselves."

Cathy shook her head emphatically. "Not true. We're two old people. Hitchers will never be suspicious of a couple of pretty young things offering them a lift." She looked pointedly at him. "Would you?"

Victor had given in. Cathy had treated both girls to a hot supper, and Victor glamoured them – hypnotically seduced them – into his service, by looking into their eyes and removing any fear or will power to fight what was to happen next. Once the girls' eyes glazed over, Victor and Cathy each took turns sucking blood from their necks, draining them *almost* dry. Then they'd had sex on the dining table, while the near-bloodless sisters sat limp beside them in the dining table chairs, watching Victor and Cathy screw, with disbelieving eyes that slowly turned red as the vampire change came over them. With the change came knowledge, and bloodlust. And sexual lust. Both girls had stripped off and joined Victor and Cathy on the table.

Covering their tracks had been easy. The next night, Judy and Laura had driven to Toledo, a town a hundred and sixty miles from Warren. There, they'd called home from a public phone, informing their worried mother that they were both fine. Then Laura had withdrawn a hundred dollars from an ATM, and bought takeout at an all-night diner, making sure they were seen, and mentioning loudly that they were driving north.

"This is Jose, uncle," Laura said. "We met him out hitching. He's looking for a job."

In response, Victor grinned, revealing bared fangs to Jose, who frowned, not quite sure what he'd seen.

"And this is Aunt Cathy," Laura added, glee in her voice.

Jose stared in horror as Cathy also bared her fangs at him. He turned to run, but Judy grabbed him and sank her fangs deep into his neck. Jose screamed.

Victor strode across and pulled Judy off Jose. Her mouth came free of the man's throat in a spurt of blood and ripped flesh.

"Wait your turn, girl!" Victor growled.

"Of course, Uncle Victor," Judy grinned, licking her bloodstained lips.

He lowered his mouth to the raw wound in Jose's neck, dug in his fangs and drank deep of the man's bleeding.

"Just don't finish him," Laura added. "I haven't had any yet."

Jose kicked weakly, not understanding what was going on. Cathy walked over and sank her teeth into the other side of Jose's neck. She sucked him deeply also, feeling her body flush with unholy vigor as his blood pumped into her mouth in warm spurts and slid down her throat.

Jose jerked and twitched between both vampires, dying slowly. He was not quite dead yet when Victor lifted his lips from his neck. Blood dribbling down his chin, he nodded to Cathy. She too withdrew her blood-smeared mouth from the dying man.

Cathy nodded to Laura and Judy. "You two can drink now."

Jose stared ahead, sightless, as the sisters, faces flush with hunger, rushed at him and fastened their mouths on his ripped-open neck, savaging it like lions attacking raw meat.

Afterwards, when Jose was well and truly drained of blood, Laura and Judy stuck a meat hook into the hole in his throat, and stuffed his corpse into the monster freezer in the dining room, suspending him by the hook.

CHAPTER 12

Invigorated by Jose's blood, Victor spent most of that night studying the document Judy and Laura had brought him from Doctor Thayer: a yellowed vellum scroll, laminated for protection against the elements. The writing on the scroll was a sequence of cryptic runes that few people alive could possibly read now. Victor was one of those few people. Most of the writing on the scroll concerned the casting of necromantic spells. Some were interesting, but for most, Victor already had alternatives that worked as well.

Momentarily, Victor remembered his old colleague, Walter Pinkman. It would have helped to have his old friend, the necromancer, to discuss his research with. But, Walter, sadly, was no more: killed by a stroke. It was arguably Walter's death that kicked off all the problems Victor experienced in Melas, as the old man handled all of Victor's day-to-day affairs in the modern world – like paying taxes and keeping the grounds around the Madison House. Once Walter died, Victor let things go unattended for a while, drawing too much attention to his affairs from outsiders.

Victor put his reminisces aside. He resumed his perusal of the extended page facing him. Now a single line jumped out at him:

'True power resides at the summoning place, there where the witches' blood was shed, where the impure were put to death.'

Victor sat a long time, letting the phrase roll through his ancient mind. 'The summoning place' clearly referred to Melas. He'd read it before in other, long destroyed tomes. Victor disliked the fact that, no matter how hard he tried to forget the town of his defeat, death and resurrection, it was impossible. There was always something that kept pushing his mind towards Melas. True, the town was a nexus of force – the blood of the many souls sacrificed there over the years had permanently desecrated it, confirming it as a permanent conduit between Earth and Hell. There were a few others situated around the United States, but Melas was the most potent.

Once again, Victor's mind leapt to Jackie Nixon, the billionaire now rebuilding the town. What did she want with it? Was she a disciple of the Master also? Was the time of the Master's return close at hand?

Victor suddenly felt unbelievably old. He studied the laminated scroll a while longer, then gave up. His thoughts were too heavy in his mind. He looked at the clock on the wall: three o'clock.

He decided to go and feed the pigs.

Downstairs, Cathy, Judy, and Laura were watching 'True Blood' on HBO. The three women were so engrossed in the episode, they didn't hear Victor's greeting as he passed them by.

Victor grimaced. It made no sense to him – vampires becoming engrossed in watching TV depictions of their lives. But just like human women, Cathy and the sisters were addicted to soap operas. Then they'd get all shrieky, whenever someone got staked.

He frowned, and then smiled. It kept them out of his hair anyway. It was either they watched TV or wanted to have sex all night.

He walked into the dining room and got Jose's body out of the freezer.

The night was cold; a cold that Victor didn't feel. Carrying Jose's body as if it was weightless, he walked to the closest of the pig enclosures. Disposing of corpses always had to be done in dead of night, when Frankie and Marv were sound asleep. True, both men had been hired for their low intellect, but Victor doubted either was so stupid as to not understand what murder was. So Victor and his vampire women always concealed the drained corpses from them. Otherwise they'd likely have to kill them to keep them quiet and then be stuck with hiring fresh hands.

Victor smiled. *People suitably stupid enough to work for a vampire are at a premium.*

Carrying Jose's frozen body by the belt like it was a suitcase, Victor pushed the pig pen door open. He smiled as he surveyed the neat rows of pens and feeder troughs. *Blood, sweet blood.*

Most of the animals were asleep, but the few that weren't whined nervously, smelling a predator in the air. Grinning, Victor walked between the aisles.

113

He became aware of a commotion in one of the pens ahead. He walked quickly, thinking that maybe a snake really had gotten in and bitten one of the sows. But no...

Victor gaped in astonishment. Frankie was facing away from Victor, unaware of his presence, but on his knees in the straw behind Bertha, Victor's prize piebald sow, fucking the pig hard. His naked thighs slammed against the sow's hairy, muddy rear.

"Ooose, Bertha. I'se gonna cum!"

The sow grunted, which made the obscene spectacle worse to Victor.

"I'se love you, girl!!! Just keep that fat pussy tight for you dada!!!"

With a loud noise, Frankie ejaculated into the pig: "Oooohhh, yeeeeeassssss, darling!"

Disgust overwhelmed Victor. Total disgust. "What the hell do you think you're doing to my pig?"

Frankie leapt up, and turned around. "Wasn't doing nuthin, Mr. Victor, hones'y. Bertha's has some itches I'se help her scratchin."

Victor looked at Bertha's behind, where a thick rope of cum was dripping from the pig's vagina. He looked at Frankie. The man's erection was drooping now; ugly and knotted all over with veins.

And to think that we've been drinking the blood from these animals! Victor thought angrily. *Damnit. I'm having a talk with Judy and Laura; I'm not taking any more 'those-hicks-are too-ugly-to-fuck' crap. If they'd been servicing these two retards, they would not have been polluting my goddam pigs!*

Victor now became aware that Frankie was looking at him oddly. "Yes, what is it?" he asked coldly. "You want my permission to screw another of my animals?"

Frankie pointed to Victor's right hand. "Who'se you'se holdin', Mr. Victor? Looks dead."

Victor groaned. "Now look here, Frankie. This isn't whatever you're thinking. This poor man had an accident and died. I want to get rid of his body."

Frankie's dumb face now creased into a sly grin. "Oh, nose, sir. He's been eatens by'se same animals was killin' you'se piggers, monts gone." He grinned, "I'se tell cops come morning."

"No need for that," Victor said, wincing. *No way am I going to convince this retard to keep his mouth shut.*

"We'se gots to, Sir," Frankie said seriously. He pointed at the corpse. "Animals killin' peoples ain't right."

Victor dropped Jose's body. "Come close, Frankie, I want to tell you a secret."

Frankie waddled closer to the pen railing, and bent over it. Once Frankie was near enough, Victor grabbed his head in both hands and cranked it sharply back, breaking his neck. Frankie fell backwards into the straw, landing on Bertha. Howling, the pig ran out from underneath his corpse, retreating into a corner and snuffling nervously.

Victor winced at the pig's noise. He reached over the railing and yanked Frankie out of the straw. Then he picked up Jose's body and made his way out of the pen, his thoughts as dark as the night.

115

Now I have TWO corpses to grind into pig feed, he thought grimly. *And I also need a good excuse to give that cretin Marv as to where Frankie's disappeared to.*

CHAPTER 13

Herman Thayer laughed. "Yes of course, Mr. Rothenstein. I have it here with me right now." He held the papyrus document his client was referring to up to the light, as if trying to see through it. "What? Oh no, sir. If I'd had it earlier, the ladies could have taken it with the last document they picked up. It just came in today. I must inform you, however, that it cost more than we agreed on; a lot more. Three hundred thousand, sir. No problem? You'll pay into my account as normal?" Herman laughed, a thick pleasant sound. "It's always a pleasure doing business with you, Mr. Rothenstein. Judy and Laura will be by shortly to pick it up? Yes, certainly, I'll be home."

Herman hung up the telephone. He dropped the document onto a woven mat on his center table. He sat facing it, occasionally observing the night skies through his living room window.

Doctor Herman Thayer was in his mid-fifties. A plump man with balding, graying hair, Dr. Thayer was Dean of Occult studies at Cleveland State University. As a sideline, he dealt in antiques, with a leaning towards the more arcane and cultic relics. Occasionally, to acquire these relics, Herman had to resort to murder. If a desired object's owner couldn't be persuaded to part with her or his property willingly,

Herman made a phone call to certain 'associates' of his, who would kill them and retrieve the desired object. Herman considered it simply business – supply and demand. An object was only safe with its owner as long as no one with a lot of money desired it. Then it must part ways with said previous owner, either by choice or duress.

Herman surveyed yet another document he'd procured for the mysterious Victor Rothenstein. Violence had been required to separate it from its previous owner. To the best of Herman's understanding, Mrs. Sara Johnston currently lay dead in her bathtub with her wrists slit, having committed suicide from inconsolable grief following the death of her husband. He smiled with thoughts of a job well done. His associates were nothing if not efficient.

The document was reputedly a stolen page from an ancient codex – the *Necronica Vampyric*.

It was nothing remarkable to look at – just a scrap of ancient papyrus, with faded hieroglyphics on one side and a translation in faded ink on the other. What *was* impressive about this papyrus fragment, however, was its age. It was believed to be thirty-five hundred years old. Herman was amused to be clutching something this ancient. Mrs. Johnston – who'd inherited it from her archeologist husband – had no idea what it was worth. She'd only refused to part from it only from sentimental value – it was left to her by her husband in his will.

Herman congratulated himself over his own business savvy. Once he'd gotten the document, he'd had its value estimated. Then he'd tripled that value when charging Mr. Rothenstein. Herman enjoyed doing business with Victor Rothenstein. The man never quibbled over price.

He smiled. Mr. R.'s female associates – Judy and Laura – would shortly arrive to collect the document. He left the room to use the toilet.

When Herman returned from relieving himself, he found a man waiting for him in his living room. The man, seated in an armchair, was middle-aged with a hard face framing cold eyes, black and menacing, like a pit bull dog that could pounce on its prey at any time.

"Who... how...?" Herman sputtered, "How did you get in here?"

The man smiled coldly. "That's not important, Dr. Thayer. What *is*, is *why* I'm here. My name is Martin Tarrant, doctor."

Herman found that he was sweating. There was something about this man that instantly put him on edge. "Okay, what do you want?"

"Simple. I want to know where Victor Rothenstein is."

"I know no one with that name," Herman blustered, certain that his tone gave him away. He did know where Victor lived. He'd been out to the farm once, and the man's number was traceable, but Herman suspected Tarrant might jeopardize his rare antique trade with Victor. That would mean a loss of millions of dollars. The man was, however, dangerous. He looked as ruthless as Pierre Marceau, the leader of Herman's murderous 'associates.'

"I don't know any Victor Rothenstein," Herman repeated coldly. "Now, if you'd *please leave.*"

Tarrant made no attempt to leave. Instead, he made himself more comfortable in the armchair, crossing his legs. He smiled thinly. "It doesn't pay to lie to me, doctor. I *know* you know Victor."

"I don't!"

"I've been monitoring your bank accounts, Dr. Thayer. Over the past month, Victor Rothenstein has made payments to you totaling a million dollars. Not directly, but through a woman named Cathy Edwards. He pays her; she pays you." He looked hard at Herman.

"That's against the law!" the doctor yelped, horrified to find himself so exposed. "You've no right. I'll call the police!"

"Shut up, doctor." Tarrant got to his feet. Herman saw that he was tall and heavily built, and carried himself with athletic ease. "True, hacking your bank transactions is against the law, but so is murdering people and stealing their valuables, isn't it?"

Tarrant's gaze fell to the papyrus fragment lying on the center table. It held his attention. It looked really ancient. He picked it up. "You steal this too, doctor?"

"Careful with that!" Herman yelled.

Tarrant smiled. "So it is valuable. Most likely filched by your people." He looked coldly at Herman. "Just tell me where Victor is, doctor, and I'll leave. I've no argument with you, or ethical qualms over how you conduct your business. All I want is an address."

Herman however was too greedy. The look in Tarrant's eyes while he'd held the papyrus fragment had convinced him the man had business interests similar to his own. He was possibly the muscle for a competitor. Yes – he had to be!

"Look," Tarrant said. "Make this easy on yourself, Doctor. I'm a reasonable man. I only resort to violence when I need to."

Herman gulped at the subtle threat. Then his resolve firmed. He wasn't letting good money end up in a competitor's pockets.

"Okay," he said. "You win. I *do* know Mr. Rothenstein, and where to find him. He lives on a pig farm near Warren." He shrugged. "But I don't know the address off-hand. It's written out on a card in my bedroom. Follow me, I'll get it for you."

"Good," Tarrant said. "Lead the way."

Herman nodded and did so. He planned to sucker Tarrant. He had a gun in his bedroom closet – a modified .25 automatic that made very little noise and wouldn't be heard outside the apartment. Once he'd shot Tarrant, he'd call Pierre Marceau to come and dispose of the body.

The only complication he foresaw was the arrival of Judy and Laura to collect Mr. Rothenstein's document. But he would be killing Tarrant in the bedroom, where the women wouldn't go. They reached the bedroom.

"Remember," Tarrant said. "Don't do anything foolish."

Herman nodded, "Of course." He pulled the closet door open, but not fully, so the other man couldn't see what he was doing. He tugged the gun out from under a pair of brown corduroy slacks, flicked off the safety and kicked the door open, sliding back the breech to prime the gun in a smooth motion. Herman fired.

Tarrant wasn't there. He looked around in surprise. Tarrant was now standing on the other side of the room, holding a pistol with an attached silencer and smiling at Herman.

"Nice try, Doctor, but you're an amateur at this."

Stupidly, Herman fired at Tarrant again. Tarrant anticipated the shot and dived out of the way, landing on Herman's huge bed. He righted himself and before the doctor could get another shot off at him, he fired, the gun making a 'pew' sound as the bullet raced toward its target.

The slug hit Herman in the gut and flung him back, slamming him into the closet. He dropped his .25 and grabbed his belly as the pain began. He looked down at the blood spreading between his fingers, then up at Tarrant, who was now climbing off the bed.

Herman's expression was astonished. "You... you..."

"You're an idiot, Doc," Tarrant said, coldly. "You'll live, though. Just call a fucking ambulance once I leave. And don't mention my name, else I'll be back to finish the job. Get it?" He kicked Herman's gun away.

Herman managed to nod. He staggered to the bed and sat down.

"Now," Tarrant said reasonably. "Let's start again. Where the hell does Victor Rothenstein live?"

Herman stared helplessly at him. His gut burnt like fire.

Tarrant rolled his eyes. "Don't be a fool, doc." He placed the silencer tip to Herman's forehead. "Or would you like me to finish the job now?"

Herman gulped and shook his head. He gave Tarrant directions to Victor's farm.

Tarrant left. On his way through Herman's living room he stopped for a moment to stare at the papyrus document again. After a moment's consideration, he decided to take it with him. He picked it up and secured it in his pocket.

It wasn't like it belonged to Dr. Thayer anyway.

Judy and Laura passed Tarrant in the hallway. He smiled at them coolly and both girls looked him over appraisingly as he headed for the front door.

"Soldier type. Looks nice and hard. Oh, I just love a man in uniform," Laura said this last loud enough for Tarrant to hear her.

"Handsome, but too old," Judy said.

"Damn," Laura whispered, "I wouldn't mind sinking my fangs into *him*."

The sisters laughed and turned the corner to Herman's apartment.

They found Herman in his living room, propped against his center table, gun in hand, a look of intense agony and consternation on his face. Judy's eyes brightened. She licked her lips at the blood trail leading from Herman to his bedroom, but both girls rushed to help Herman up.

"He stole it," he gasped at the sisters.

"Who stole what?"

"A man stole Mr. Rothenstein's document!" Herman calmed himself through his pain. Sweat was

123

pouring from his brow. "A tall man called Tarrant... just now..." Some instinct prevented him from mentioning that Tarrant had been asking for Victor. "He shot me and took your boss's paper."

"Hard-faced, like a cop or soldier?"

Herman nodded feverishly.

"We passed him outside," Judy said. She looked at her sister, and asked, "Go after him?"

"He's armed!" Herman whispered.

Both girls looked at him with a peculiar expression on their faces.

"Oh, guns aren't a bother," Judy said. She winked at her sister.

"Forget the damn document," Laura told Judy. "Victor's always buying some arcane shit or other. Sooner or later, he'll find something else he likes."

She smiled at Herman, a predator's glint in her eyes. "More important, Doctor, is what do we do about you?"

"That's obvious," Herman wheezed. "Get me to a hospital so I don't bleed to death. I need a fucking doctor."

Judy licked her lips. The blood oozing out of the front of Herman's shirt was making her dizzy. The smell of it filled her nose, making it hard for her to think clearly. She looked at her sister, and Laura had the same glazed look in her eyes.

"We drink him, then?" Judy asked.

Laura nodded, "Yeah, but Victor sure will be pissed."

Judy shook her head. "We'll just tell him the doctor was almost dead and we didn't want to waste him."

Laura nodded. They turned to look at Herman, who was staring at them in incomprehension.

"Please take me to hospital," he pleaded. "You've a car, haven't you?"

In response, both girls bared their fangs at him. Herman froze in horror. Then, realizing what the girls were, he raised his gun and began firing at them. The repeated crack of the .25 in the apartment sounded like twigs breaking.

Judy and Laura giggled as the bullets punched holes through their bodies: holes that to Herman's horror didn't bleed. Both walked calmly toward him as the gun clip clicked empty.

"See, doctor," Laura said, "we weren't lying earlier – guns really don't bother us."

Both girls leapt on top of Herman. Judy ripped his shirt apart and buried her mouth in the blood pouring from his belly. She dug her fingers into the bullet hole and ripped it open wide, burying her head in his gut and lapping up his spurting blood.

Herman screamed, so Laura clouted him to shut him up. He floundered like a fish on the living room floor, but weakly battered Judy's head with his gun to make her stop. Laura grabbed his gun-hand and gripping his forearm in her other hand, bent Herman's hand back till his wrist shattered with a noise like a gunshot.

Then, while Herman sputtered helplessly, Laura sank her fangs into the soft white flesh of his throat, ripping out his voice box, so he could no longer scream. She relaxed, and sucked the sweet warm blood out of Herman. Blood that intoxicated her like a deeply fermented wine as it trickled down into her belly.

***

"What do you mean, stolen?" raged Victor, when the girls returned, giggling and satiated with blood.

Judy shrugged, "Dunno. Some guy just turned up – just before we got there, shot Thayer, and left with the paper."

"Yeah, poor Thayer," smirked Laura, licking her lips. "Such a shame it was too late for him."

"But not for you, it seems," snapped Victor in disgust.

Judy and Laura tried to suppress giggles, holding onto one another as if they were drunk.

Judy made doe-eyes at Victor, "But so much warm blood... just... gushing out. On tap. You wouldn't have been able to resist it yourself, *Uncle!*"

But Victor's mind was already too absorbed in wondering who exactly this 'guy' was, and what he wanted with the *Necronica Vampyric*. And what this event meant for themselves.

CHAPTER 14

The two jeeps pulled up to the farm gates at noon.

"Here we are," Tarrant said. He gestured to one of his men, "Open the gate."

The man, a young blond-haired ex-marine, leapt down and unbolted the gate. There were eight of them in the two Jeeps: Tarrant, William, and Kate, and five of Tarrant's men, all hard as nails by the look of them.

"I really wish you hadn't come along," William told Kate as their vehicles rolled down the approach to the farmhouse. "Best you were safe at home."

Kate grinned, "Too late for that now." She shivered, so William saw she wasn't as confident as she portrayed herself.

Tarrant shared William's opinion of Kate's involvement. "Remember to remain outside the house, Kate. My men will hand the baby over to you once it's located. If for any reason, you must enter the farmhouse, keep behind my men." He smiled his ugly smile. "This is for your own protection."

Kate nodded, "Thanks. I'll do as you say."

They pulled up to the stone farmhouse and disembarked. Tarrant's mercenaries unloaded from their vehicles special equipment that William purchased for this task: two bundles of two-feet-long wooden stakes, their ends whittled to wicked points. There was also a pile of stout hammers that one of the men distributed to everyone, William and Kate included.

William had told Terrant before leaving that during his first experience with Rothenstein, the vampire was not the only vampire they found, and due care should be given should circumstances be similar.

All the men wore flak jackets and SWAT helmets, with protective face grills, holstered pistols and knives. In addition, they wore protective crosses, and each carried a flask of water that William had blessed.

William looked around. The farm was a lovely rustic setting in the bright noonday sun, an endless expanse of green that stretched off to a distant horizon of trees, above which the clouds looked like balls of cotton.

"Such a lovely place," Kate said, echoing his thoughts. "That far countryside looks like a painted landscape. I'd love to own a place like this someday."

William nodded, "Utter beauty." *And now totally defiled*, he thought angrily. Once William added Victor to the perfect picture, all the rural beauty around them counted for nothing. The vampire was a blot on the beauty of God's creation that had to be erased. For good, now.

We made a mistake last time, he thought. *This time I'm doing it right. I only hope my cousin's still alive in there.*

William was dressed in his priest's cassock, complete with white collar. From some sense of perversion, before they'd left to join up with Tarrant and his men, Kate had insisted that they fuck with his clerical garb on.

"Oh no," William had said. "What is it with you and defrocking priests?"

She'd grinned, "You were already defrocked when I met you."

William searched for an answer to that. Kate had pulled up his robe, pulled down his pants, and taken him in her mouth, sucking him hard till William had abandoned his reservations about having sex with a vampire at the door, and carried her over to their bed.

The sex had been hard and fast and wonderful. Kate had come, screaming and biting her lips. Afterward, he saw that he'd gotten semen on the cassock. *Oh fucking no*, he thought. He was less upset over the mess than the fact that it didn't bother him as much as he felt it should.

Damn, he thought. *Am I really this far from God? Does the Almighty's grace really count for nothing any longer?*

Kate had giggled at his apoplexy. She'd climbed out of bed and got a tissue.

"This is a holy garment," William complained as she cleaned off the cum-smear.

"Not anymore. Really, darling, you'd be better off wearing jeans. You're likely to trip up in this."

Her comment summarized William's issues over bringing Kate along with him. She still showed no gravity about the severity of the situation. Kate apparently viewed this vampire hunt as a scenario from a Hollywood horror flick – merely play-acting. Now, with a cloud of darkness settling on his soul despite the

129

bright sun, he wasn't so sure he didn't too. Who else ever defiled themselves before tackling evil?

William pushed away his depression. It was done – too late now to cry over spilt milk, or in this case, cum. It was good that they had the element of surprise on their side. No way would the vampire be expecting William, even by himself, never mind with six other men with stakes. He smiled. Yes, this would be over soon. His cousin would be rescued and he and Kate would be able to resume their everyday lives again.

He smiled at Kate. Her returning grin said it all: *And one million dollars richer.*

But for William, it wasn't about the money.

William looked over to his right, at the pig enclosures. The three huge buildings looked like mirror blocks, the high sun glittering brightly off their metal roofs. Through an opening of the nearest building he made out the penned swine. Their loud grunting easily crossed the distance.

William also saw a solitary face peering out through the glass at them.

"Someone's watching us," he told Tarrant.

Tarrant dispatched one of his men to find out whoever it was. The mercenary jogged off, but was back shortly, dragging behind him a short man in dirty overalls. William was appalled by how ugly the man was, with a huge hairy mole on his left cheek.

"I'm Tarrant," Tarrant said. "I'm here to see Victor about buying some pigs."

"Ma name's Marv," the ugly man replied. "You'se cain't see Mr. Victor and the missus now. They don't see no visitors before seven's evening. Best you'se comes back then."

Tarrant looked at William, with a raised eyebrow. "The missus? Victor's married?"

Marv nodded, with a broad idiotic grin. His rheumy eyes turned dreamy. "Missus Cathy, sir. Real beautiful she are, toose."

"Tell me, Marv," Tarrant said quietly. "How many people live here? I mean, other than Mr. Victor and his wife?"

"Jus 'em, 'n 'em two gals, Judy 'n Laura."

Tarrant nodded. "Four," he told his men.

That's three more than we planned for, William thought. He felt sudden dismay. This already wasn't going according to plan. He tried to rally himself, to take refuge in faith. *I need to be strong now, but already I've hindered myself with the sins of the flesh. Lord, help me.* But God seemed far off, a distant cold judge, not the loving father and comforting presence of the Holy Spirit William had once loved and reveled in.

Unable to find divine succor, William looked helplessly at Tarrant. "We need to rethink this," he whispered harshly. "Four is three more than we planned for."

"We've enough stakes," Kate said.

William spun round to rebuke her, but found he couldn't. Her impish smile as she looked back at him totally disarmed him. *She just doesn't get it,* William thought in utter disbelief. *She really doesn't get the danger here, that we could all be dead in a matter of minutes.*

He shook his head at Kate, then turned his attention to Tarrant. The ex-soldier was deep in thought, scratching his leathered jaw, his brow furrowed with deep concentration.

"Kate's right," he said finally. "We have enough stakes. We just need to adjust our tactics a bit, leave two covering the exit."

Marv now saw that the men were all unsmiling, their faces grim with purpose. He also noticed the sharpened stakes Tarrant and his men carried.

"What dose for?" he asked, pointing at the stakes, his ugly face suddenly very suspicious.

"Pig business," William improvised. "Mr. Victor made enquiries how to restrain his pigs outside their enclosure. We're here for a demonstration." For emphasis, he pushed the pointed end of a stake into the grass, and hammered it down.

Marv chortled, spit running from the corner of his mouth, "That ain't keep no porks in! They'se steps over its easy!"

William looked at the two-foot pole. Marv was telling the truth.

Kate came to his rescue. She smiled disarmingly at Marv and explained: "It's for piglets. L'il porkers."

William was amazed at the authenticity of her southern accent. She sounded purebred Texan.

Marv nodded, thinking hard. "Yeah, dat's boutta right size for dose l'il uns."

Tarrant checked his watch. "Time to get to work." He looked at Marv, his eyes cold. "Okay, thanks for all your help. We'll go in to talk to Victor, now. You can get back to work."

"Oh, nose, sir," Marv said, his mole twitching like a rat smelling the air as his face crinkled up in alarm, "Mr. Victor, he's gon' fire me if you bothers him 'fore night. Just like he fired Frankie. Frankie done been sexing Mr. Victor's pigs and…"

Tarrant smiled coldly. "He isn't going to fire you, Marv, or anyone else. Trust me."

He turned to walk off, but Marv grabbed his hand to restrain him. "Mister…"

Tarrant scowled and nodded to his men. Two of them immediately grabbed Marv.

"Lemme go!" Marv yelped. "You'se caint disturb Mr. Victor!"

"Shut him up!" Tarrant ordered.

The resulting punch to the solar plexus shut Marv up good. He wheezed and puffed, drooling spit down his overalls.

"Put him back with his pigs," Tarrant said coldly.

The men dragged Marv off between them. William watched him go with some misgiving, Marv's unintelligible protests floating back to them. At the pig enclosure, one of the men hit Marv another hard punch to the gut, then pushed him through the door. William winced as Marv's pained yelp reached them. The mercenaries shut the door on Marv and the two men jogged back over to Tarrant.

"Okay, let's do this," Tarrant told William and Kate.

He gave the signal and the mercenaries made their way to the front door, forcing it open with a pry bar.

Marv peered angrily out at the men breaking into his master's house. *Damn burgulers*, he thought angrily, *I'se gon' shows 'em!* The pain in his gut was making him breathe in short breaths. Marv knew he was ugly and dumb, but he also knew burglars when he saw them. *And damn, yes, these be burgulers, sure as ma cock's pink*, he thought.

Wheezing with each step, Marv made his way down the aisle of pigs. His gut felt like he was about to shit. He paused momentarily by Bertha's cage, where the piebald sow lifted her head from her feed and looked at Marv. Marv thought the pig's expression was accusatory, like it was asking: 'Where's Frankie? Where's ma darlin' Frankie?'

Marv chortled, "Sorry, Berthie, Frankie done get the sack cos he loves you too much. I'se warns him to stop fuckin' ya, but he ain't ever listens to me. So's Mr. Victor done fired him." He scratched the pig behind her ears. "Is true, girl, I just wakes up and he's done left for Nevada. Didn' even pack ees things."

Bertha snorted and stuck her snout back into the trough of pigswill. Marv shrugged. *What's I'se to dooes? I done told Frankie ta stop porkin' Mr. Victor's pork, but he says he's gotta cum inna pussy not inna his hand.*

Marv was pleased about one thing though over the whole 'Frankie firing' incident. *An' now looks*, he thought, his thoughts jumbling happily in his head. *Now, Missus Cathy done now ordered Judy and Laura to fuck us hands twice a week, minimum. Woooeee!*

134

In fact Marv had screwed the sisters last night. Or rather, they'd screwed him. Marv's penis still hurt from the amount of sex they'd demanded of him.

"Yassir," he said out loud. "Def'nly pays ta be patient-like. If Frankie's lissen ta me, wees both be humping the gals now."

Marv stole a quick look out through the barn door of the pig house. The burglars had now jimmied the door open and were standing talking.

They'se ain't no damn pig-farmers ta be actin all saspicious like 'at, Marv thought. *They'se burgulers alright.*

He'd now reached the far end of the pig aisles. Here there was an office, with a telephone connected to the main house. Marv ignored the phone, however. It only ever worked at night. For some reason, no matter how long he let it ring in the daytime, no one ever answered. It was like the house was dead then. Instead, he pulled open the table drawer. Inside it was a red buzzer switch with a cord running behind it, underneath the table.

"Now, boys," 'Mr. Victor' had told Marv and Frankie when they'd both begun working here. "I want you both to listen close and remember this."

He'd indicated the buzzer. "Now, don't ever push this unless it's an emergency."

"Emer . . ." Frankie couldn't get his mind around the idea of the word.

"Emergency," Victor repeated. "That means danger. Things like burglars or fire." He'd looked intently at the pair. "Also remember, don't push it at night, only during the day."

"Daytime?" Frankie had grinned stupidly. "Whyzat, boss? Thought burglars steals at nat."

Victor nodded. "Yes, daytime. Sometimes I work overnight and sleep deeply." He frowned. "Now, if either of you see anyone suspicious around here during the daytime, for instance someone who insists on seeing me, and refuses to wait for a night appointment, you come right here immediately and push this buzzer, okay?"

Both men had nodded.

"Remember, you do it immediately," Victor repeated.

Now Marv looked at the red button. *Yassir, I gon' teach 'em darn burgulers a good lessin 'n r'spect.* He pressed the red button, holding his stubby finger down on it long so that Mr. Victor would be especially annoyed at having his sleep disturbed. Marv looked out the window one last time. All the burglars had now entered the house. Marv left the office grinning broadly. *Darn creeps gon' get a right tell'n off, fa sure, nowse.*

CHAPTER 15

The farmhouse interior was dim. All the blinds were drawn and the only lighting came from sunbeams peering around the heavy curtains. Kate found the light switch and flicked it on, looking around the front room. It had an older but polished hardwood floor and sturdy oak furniture.

"Appears Amish," she commented to no one in particular. "Looks normal enough."

William looked at Tarrant and the mercenaries and gestured around the front room. "They'll be down in the basement," he said. "This electric light doesn't hurt them, but vampires don't like being this close to the sun. One flick of a drape and they start burning."

Tarrant nodded. He called two men over. "You two, stay up here with Kate. Check the house for the baby."

"Yes, Major."

Tarrant turned to William. "Down to the basement then." Back to his men, he ordered, "Remember not to get bitten. Drive the stakes clean through the heart. Let's keep this a clean, efficient operation."

He flicked on his helm-light. All the others did the same, each man gripping a stake in one hand and a hammer in the other.

"Take care, darling," Kate said, as the five of them walked toward the basement door.

They went down.

William pointed to the runes inscribed in blood on the basement door. "They're in here, for sure."

Tarrant gave a silent signal to his men and one slowly pushed the basement door open, carefully, so as to keep its creaking to a minimum. The basement was spacious, with stone walls. A side door led off the main room to what seemed to be a store, with wall shelves.

William nodded. "Vampires like stone around them. Light doesn't get through it, no matter what."

"Any signs of the baby?" Tarrant asked the blond Marine at the far side of the room.

"No," he replied.

There were four ebony coffins down in the basement. All were open, their white silk upholstery fluorescent in the helmet lamp-light. The open caskets sent an instant note of warning to William. "Something's wrong!" he told Tarrant.

Tarrant and his men quickly walked across to inspect the four coffins. "They're all empty," Tarrant said, looking at William. "You said–"

"They're not upstairs," William interrupted him. "They're down here somewhere. We need to be careful, or–"

Tarrant shushed him with a finger to his lips. He nodded to two of his men and gestured to the store-room. Hammers and stakes held ready, both men padded to the door and looked in. For the briefest of moments all was silent, then: "It's a trap!"

The mercenary in the rear who'd yelled the warning was knocked flying by a huge bat bursting out of the store room.

The other man sank to the floor, gibbering, blinded, his eyes pools of blood. The monster descended with him, shrouding his body in its leathern wings as it ripped out his throat. The man's hammer and stake fell uselessly from his fingers.

Two more bats followed the first two out of the store room. Pandemonium broke loose.

No, no, no! William thought as one of the bats landed on his chest, attempting to bite him. Unable to stake the creature at such close range, he knocked it off him with the hammer he held.

The bat crashed to the floor and transformed into Cathy Edwards. William thought she looked familiar, but had no time to fix recognition in his mind.

Cathy was off the floor in a flash and at him again, her hands crooked into claws, her mouth a cavern of yawning fangs. Her eyes were mirrors of rage and bloodlust. William couldn't evade her charge, and as she knocked him off his feet, they went down together in a heap, with her on top of him, scratching at his eyes to rip them out of his head.

William gripped her wrists and held her far enough off him, so that she couldn't get her fangs to his throat. Her spittle dribbled down on him, viscid and pungent.

William began: "I rebuke you, in nomine Chr…"

But Cathy kneed him in the groin before he could finish the incantation. William winced, kicking her off him. Before she leapt at him again, he hurriedly looked around at the others. The bat that had blinded the first

139

mercenary was now rising up from the man's drained corpse, transforming into Victor Rothenstein as it stood.

Then Cathy Edwards barreled into William again and he was fighting for his life, too engrossed with surviving the vampire's onslaught to think about any of the others, wondering how everything had gone so wrong so quickly.

Martin Tarrant was also fighting for his life. Judy had him pinned against the wall and was raking at his eyes with stiffened fingers. Tarrant looked into the young blonde's beautiful face and winced at the primal hunger reflected there. He felt no human kinship. She was an animal, a ravening beast; nothing else, closer to a wolf than a person.

Conditioned by a lifetime of combat to expect the unexpected, Tarrant hadn't dropped his stake and hammer when the vampires had surprised him and his men and gripped both implements firmly, realizing that his survival depended on them. He was, however, unable to use either as they'd planned. Instead, he brandished the stake between himself and Judy to prevent the vampiress reaching his throat while he smashed her head with the hammer. But the damage he did made no difference to the ferocity of her attack. Even as Tarrant ripped opened holes in her face, Judy flailed wildly against him, biting at the hand wielding the hammer. Her spittle smacked his face with viscous goo, stinging his eyes. It entered his mouth as he pushed her back.

Tarrant saw that his men were all involved in similar life-and-death struggles. William was also rolling around on the floor, entangled with a black-clad brunette atop him, the brunette's fangs snapping at him like a dog. The basement resounded with the sound of desperate fighting and the vampire's bestial yells. Coming to apprehend Victor Rothenstein, Tarrant hadn't expected anything like this.

Tarrant returned to his own desperate struggle with Judy. For all his extensive battle experience, Tarrant was horrified. The vampiress attacking him was incredibly strong – much stronger than any man he'd ever fought before. Once again, he was unable to divorce her similarity to a rabid animal, her red eyes, like pools of blood, reinforcing that impression.

Tarrant whacked the hammer into Judy's forehead. Howling with rage, she smashed her fist against Tarrant's hammer-hand. He screamed in pain as his forearm shattered from the impact and he dropped the hammer. Slowly, Judy forced her face closer and closer to his, her jaws yawning open. Tarrant's broken arm hung useless by his side. He fought against the pain, seeking a way to save himself.

Tarrant's heavy silver cross had swung on its chain to the back of his neck in the struggle, and his hands had been busy with the stake he was fending Judy off with. He'd earlier noticed her avoiding the crucifix, and during those few times she'd seen it, she'd flinched as if she'd been burnt. In a last desperate move, Tarrant summoned all his strength and dropped the stake separating him and Judy. Flinching as his broken forearm bones rubbed together, he pushed her off him in a last desperate rush of strength and wrenched his neck chain off, gripping the cross.

As the vampiress closed in on him again, Tarrant stabbed her in the head with the cross. She screamed, her mouth gaping open in an 'o' of frustrated rage; then she staggered back from him, fire spurting from her head. Tarrant watched, horrified, while the flames burnt down from Judy's head to consume her whole body. In mere moments the vampire was a pile of smoking white ash.

Tarrant looked down at his broken right arm, bent at an awkward angle, with blood dripping down through his fingers. He grimaced at the pain coursing up through it.

One of Tarrant's men broke away from the general confused melee and rushed to his side and asked, "Are you okay, sir?"

"Look out!" Tarrant yelled. The warning came too late.

Like a bolt of lightning, Laura leapt up on the man's back, sinking her teeth deep into his neck. The man tried hitting her with his stake, but she was behind him.

"Use your cross!" Tarrant yelled.

The mercenary tried to, but Laura batted his hand away from the holy relic. Then she bit out his throat, his blood spurting like a fountain all over Laura's face and hair.

Tarrant dropped to his knees and began fumbling through Judy's ash for his cross. *Fuck, where is it?* he thought desperately, as Laura ripped the mercenary's head clean off his shoulders and flung it across the room to where Victor was engaged with two of Tarrant's men advancing on him, gripping their stakes like spears.

The decapitated corpse in front of Tarrant collapsed to the ground, a bloody mess pumping out blood. Barefoot, Laura stomped through the blood. "You die now!" she hissed at Tarrant.

Tarrant's scrabbling fingers found the cross amidst Judy's ashes, wedged in a crack in the floor. Try as he might he couldn't free it with only his left hand. He looked over at the headless corpse lying on his front, covering his own cross.

Unable to free the cross, Tarrant looked around for his stake instead.

William knew Victor's only hope was to fight and win. It was afternoon outside – there was no chance of him fleeing the farmhouse. William winced as Cathy Edward's nails raked down his cheek. The wound was shallow, but burnt like fire. He and Cathy were now rolling around on the floor, him doing his best to keep her mouth away from his throat. He still had hold of her wrists, but it was hard going, because as a supernatural being, the vampire was much stronger than he was.

"You're going to die here, priest!" she spat at him.

Cathy leaned in close to William's face, her fangs mere inches from him. William's cross too had swung around behind his back during their endless rolling to-and-fro across the floor. He head-butted her and she reeled back, stunned, then leaned in again, her eyes hungrier than before.

William got one arm under Cathy's chin to push her head away. With his other hand, he freed the bottle of holy water and flung it onto Cathy Edwards.

"In nomine Christi," he pronounced as it poured over the vampire woman.

She sputtered in horror on realizing what he'd poured on her, and the implication of it. Then, in surprise the vampire realized that nothing bad was happening to her.

"That's *ordinary* water, priest," she sneered at William. "Try something else."

William gaped at the vampire in horror, his thoughts in a tumult. *Ordinary water? Ordinary? But I blessed it... I blessed it!*

Victor was held up against the wall by two of Tarrant's men who were herding him with stakes. The vampire looked furious, his horrible mouth and fangs red with the blood of his first victim. He looked around the room, cerise eyes quickly taking in the situation. He'd cursed when Judy was stabbed in the head with the crucifix. *Damn!*

Victor was pleased, however that Marv had had sufficient presence of mind to sound the alarm and rouse him and his women before these interlopers arrived. Otherwise they'd have been helpless. Now it was a fair fight with the vampire hunters.

He looked at the two men holding stakes on him. Both were clearly scared behind their cold expressions. *And well you should be scared, cowards,* he thought. *You're nothing but food in the presence of a being much greater than you.* He reared up to attack the men, who shrank away from him.

The men's behavior was strange, however. Though keeping him at bay with their sharpened stick and crosses – *Damn*, he hated crosses and silver – they made no further attempt to attack him and deal a finishing blow. Their eyes said they were playing for time, were waiting for someone. Maybe the older man, the one who'd killed Judy.

Victor took advantage of the men's hesitation. Neither had any true idea what they were facing. The priest tangling with Cathy might have, but he would soon die too.

"Die!" Victor screamed at the mercenaries. He leapt between them both. They immediately swung their stakes to block him off. Victor used his superior speed, smashing the men's stakes aside. The force spun the men themselves sideways, permitting Victor to get between them, and then behind them.

Both men spun backward, looking for him. Victor quickly broke the neck of the one on the right, then slammed the dead body into his companion's stake as he thrust it at Victor, then he yanked the man in close and ripped out his throat. He thrilled deliciously at the terror in the man's eyes as he killed him. He drank deep of the man's blood, then dropped his corpse.

He looked around the room surveying the combat, seeking the leader of these invaders of his privacy.

Tarrant located his stake, which lay in the headless mercenary's blood to Laura's left.

Laura sneered at Tarrant. "I'm going to bleed you dry, you son-of-a-bitch. You'll die just like he did."

The vampire woman leapt at Tarrant, who rushed for the stake. Laura guessed his intent and cut him off, kicking Tarrant's broken arm to discourage him so he howled in pain, but he grabbed the stake anyway. He raised it and faced Laura, blood dripping from the sharpened wood pole.

The pair began circling each other, in the enclosed space. Laura kept on Tarrant's right, trying to get behind his wounded arm, while Tarrant tried unsuccessfully to get a clear sight of her left breast so he could impale her.

Laura's attention was being distracted by William and Cathy smashing into her from behind, the pair hitting and slashing at each other furiously. Tarrant slowly forced the vampire away from him, backing her across the room, until Laura was unbalanced by stumbling over a corpse, and knocked off her feet, toppling into one of the open caskets.

Before she could recover herself, Tarrant was on her. He slammed the stake down into her chest, and then leaned all his weight on it, forcing it through her left breast into her heart.

Beneath him, Laura's look or rage turned to one of dread and horror.

Tarrant grinned coldly, "Say hi to them in hell for me, bitch!"

He kept his weight on the stake, while the vampire woman withered away to a wizened, emaciated corpse. The pine casket caught fire. Tarrant leapt back from it, wheezing from the effort. Gasping with relief, he watched the casket incinerate.

Then he heard loud breathing behind him. He spun around, to see Victor facing him. The vampire's expression was one of intense rage, the cords of his neck stood out taut with his immense anger.

"How dare you attack me, you human worm?" Victor screamed at Tarrant. He suddenly swelled, increasing in size, becoming more bestial, apelike rather than human.

Tarrant stared the vampire down. "You come with me," he spat back. His voice, however, lacked any conviction. He could see that all his men were now dead and William was still occupied.

"We'll see about that," Victor said. Slowly, confidently, Victor stalked towards Tarrant, relishing the man's fear.

Tarrant carefully backed away from the vampire, eyes wildly scanned the room, looking for a cross or stake. There were none. Then Tarrant remembered his flask of holy water hanging there at his belt – his possible salvation in this situation. While keeping his eyes on the approaching Victor, he fumbled the flask off his hip and tried to open it up.

Victor realized what was in the flask, rushing at Tarrant and savagely knocking the flask out of his grip, so it sailed away over the remaining caskets. Tarrant now had three broken fingers on his *good* hand.

Victor laughed as the man winced with the pain. "You're done for, human. You're already broken, and I'll finish off the job!"

Tarrant looked around wildly for a means of escape. He found none. The monster vampire grabbed him. After first breaking Tarrant's left arm, so he couldn't fight back, Victor bent the yelling Tarrant over, into one of the open coffins.

"Help me, William!" Tarrant screamed, kicking desperately. His broken arm flapped uselessly by his side.

"William?" The name rang an alarm bell in Victor's head. But he looked down at the priest still rolling around on the floor with Cathy, the man's face veiled by Cathy's hair. Clearly, he'd shortly be dead, too.

"No help there for you," he told the desperate Tarrant. "Now I feed on you."

"Nooooo!"

Victor clouted Tarrant a hard blow to the forehead to stop him flailing. Then he bent to the dazed man's neck and sank his teeth into the pale throat-flesh, with its lovely throbbing veins. Tarrant jerked as if he was having a fit, while Victor calmly drained all the blood out of him.

William had quickly gotten over the fact that his 'holy' water was useless against Cathy. He had no idea how he'd overlooked blessing this single flask, but had no time for reflection. Cathy Edwards was on him, sticking to him like glue and William was tiring fast. Their fight had taken them across the basement and back again, rolling, staggering up and toppling together over corpses.

The vampire was unbelievably strong. Her eyes like hungering blood specks in her bone-white visage, Cathy forced herself closer and closer against William. Her breath poured over him, like the stench from a sewer full of rotting corpses.

"Feed me!" she shrieked, lunging in so close her lips brushed William's chin. He managed to push her off before she bit, however.

I can't keep this up for much longer, William thought in desperation. *God, help me!* But God still seemed far off, distant as a star.

Almost as confirmation, William's cross now become irretrievably tucked down into the rear of the neck of his cassock, wedged tight there – unable to shake loose. With both his hands gripping his vampire assailant's wrists, William was powerless to retrieve it.

They toppled together over a corpse, crashing down hard side by side. Looking up, William saw Victor bent over Tarrant's body, half stuffed in a casket. The vampire's hair was red with the dying man's blood. He also caught sight for the first time of the buzzer over the basement door that had flashed Marv's warning to the vampires when they'd arrived.

Then Cathy was atop him again, fangs once more questing for his throat. William fended her off with desperation now. His glimpse of the room had also updated him of the fact that only three of them – himself, Cathy and Victor – remained alive.

He needed to deal with Cathy before Victor was done slaking his thirst, since he couldn't tackle both vampires at once.

Fortune appeared to smile on William. He spotted Tarrant's cross, still wedged in the gap in the floor where it had gotten stuck. It was a short distance from Cathy's head, but intent on sinking her teeth into William, she hadn't noticed it.

With herculean effort, William pushed them both toward the cross, covering them both with dirt and shed blood. Letting go of her wrists, William gripped Cathy's neck and shoved her head hard against the cross.

At the contact, Cathy's cheek caught fire. Flames spurting from her face, she screamed and leapt off William. Her milk-white cheek now sported a deep red gash, her flesh smoking as she expressed her horror and fear, her breath coming in gasps. She looked around to see what had burnt her and saw the cross, wedged in its hole in the floor. William was now fighting to wrest it free, but like Tarrant, was unable to.

Snarling, Cathy flung herself at him, certain that she'd kill him now. William was faster, though. He'd quickly realized the cross wouldn't jerk free, and looked around for an alternate attack or defense.

Behind them both, Victor slurped deep at Tarrant's throat, with nary a glance in their direction. William's eyes now fell on the decapitated mercenary's stake, lying in the man's blood. He grabbed it as Cathy flew at him, turning it so that its point aimed at her chest.

Rushing at speed, Cathy was unable to avoid the stake. She landed on it, its point stabbing deep into her breast. She began thrashing and screaming. Even as Cathy impaled herself on the stake, William was already up and forcing it at her with all his might, ensuring it penetrated her all the way through. Cathy Edwards exploded into flame.

Only two of us left now, William thought, as the vampire woman burnt to ash. He spun around to face Victor.

Cathy's anguished screaming had aroused Victor from his blood feast, and he, too, turned as William did. They saw one another's faces directly for the first time, and Victor froze as he recognized William.

Anger flared in the vampire's eyes. "You!" he spat at William. "I should have known it was you!" The rage in his voice was mixed with fear – a dread in remembrance that it was William and his friends who'd killed his last host.

William scowled, but made no reply. Victor was a horror to behold now. The front of his chest was stained red, as was the lower half of his face. William now saw what Tarrant meant: this was by no means the same Victor, he'd once faced. This man was younger, spryer – but such adjectives meant nothing. *A vampire is a supernatural being,* he reminded himself. *Even a vampire child is strong enough to lift a horse.* His myriad of bruises from his fight with the vampire woman, Cathy Edwards, bore testament to his knowledge.

William and Victor faced each other across the mess of corpses and blood. Neither made any attempt to cross to the other. William freed the cross stuck in his collar, ripping it off his throat and holding it up, nodding satisfaction at the fear of the holy object that instantly flew into the vampire's eyes. But at the same

151

time, William, too, was scared. He had no wish to die again. He felt too far away from the Almighty, and lacked any confidence of his final destination when he shut his eyes that final time. William had seen Hell in all its horror – and had no desire to reside there permanently. William understood that Victor was scared of him, but this stalemate couldn't last forever. He needed to attack Victor first, before the vampire rallied. Keeping his eyes on Victor, he bent and picked up the stake he'd killed Cathy with. His thoughts momentarily leapt to Kate. *The baby? Has she found it?* He straightened up again.

"You killed my entire family – you god-forsaken abomination," he said quietly. "This is payback."

William thought he saw a flicker of surprise leap into Victor's eyes at his statement. Then his thoughts changed to those of vengeance and he charged Victor, leaping across the bloody patches of floor.

For a moment Victor stood his ground. He bristled, the cord in his neck taut as he prepared to leap at William. Then his nerve broke: a combination of factors – the irresistible, searing, divine heat of the cross held by the charging priest; the knowledge of the stake's fatality; but most of all memory, cursed memory of his last defeat broke his nerve. Covering his eyes from the holy white fire spurting from the cross, Victor ducked out of William's way and ran for the stairwell door.

Upstairs, upstairs! he thought desperately. *It is still daytime but the house is darkened.*

Altering his form into that of a monster bat again, he flew up the stairs.

With Victor no longer where he'd been, William skidded to a halt on a patch of blood and slammed into a wall. He spun around, to see his quarry disappearing out of the basement door. William's anger was instantly replaced with fear.

Kate, he thought. *Kate's upstairs and she's not expecting someone as powerful as him.*

He rushed across the basement and ascended the stairs after Victor.

CHAPTER 16

William burst through the upper staircase door.

Damn! he exclaimed in distress, looking around in dismay at the blood everywhere. Victor had clearly caught the sentries by surprise. One of them was headless, his corpse draped over a table. The man's head lay across the room from him, under a chair. His stake and hammer lay under the table that bore his corpse. William noted with relief that the dead mercenary was only one corpse in the room. Then he heard a snuffling sound coming from the living room off to his left, and a scared yelp.

Kate.

William turned to run in there, but noticed the headless man's flask of holy water dangling over the end of the table, swinging on its cord. He quickly freed it from the corpse's belt. Feeling more confident now that he could attack his foe from a distance, he rushed into the dining room.

The dining room blinds were all shut, the room lighted by a crystal chandelier. William immediately saw the second mercenary, who staggered around the room, desperately swatting at the monstrous bat that ripped at him with tooth and claw. In desperation equivalent to the wounded man's, William looked around for Kate.

He saw her and sighed his relief. Kate was unharmed. She was crouched in the crevice between Victor's monstrous refrigerator and a large crockery cabinet. She gripped her cross and stake tightly. William's heart sank on seeing that Kate didn't have a baby with her, and despite it being her yelp that had summoned him, the expression on Kate's face was one of excitement more than fear.

Damn, William thought, *she really does look like she's in a movie theatre.* He now realized that Kate's yelp had been that of a filmgoer – someone startled by an unexpected death in a suspenseful movie. Kate saw William and nodded at him, her face white with emotion, then immediately turned her attention back to the man fighting the giant bat.

She's totally enthralled in this, William thought. *She's too scared to help the victim, and too excited to flee.*

William turned from his girlfriend to address the vampire. Still in bat form, Victor was now perched on the man's shoulders, fangs deep in his head. Blood poured from the man's face from the paired wounds of previous bites. The man still fought, hitting the bat with his hammer, his stake long abandoned as ineffectual at such close range. Bat and man twirled around the room in a macabre dance, both bloodstained. William saw the man's eyes, which blinked dully at him, the mind behind them already receding down into the caverns of death. It was clearly already too late to save the man. Even if he survived

Victor's attack, he would still need to be staked to prevent him from transforming into a vampire.

But first, the bat. Stake and cross raised high, William rushed across the room, yelling. As he charged, his eyes met the bat's cold soulless rubies filled with only thirst for human blood. William brought the stake down, but the bat took to the air and the stake plunged into the bleeding man's neck and down into his chest.

Behind William, the bat became Victor again. The vampire spun William around and backhanded him, causing William to drop the cross and fly through the air. He landed on the dining table, knocking a bowl of fruit to the floor. Kate screamed, in real terror now.

Victor turned to look at her, and laughed. "Once I kill *him*, I'm coming for you, woman. You'll be the replacement for my dead lovers."

Kate stared at Victor, white-faced. He turned back to William, who had now picked himself up using the table for support. He launched himself through the air at the vampire, landing on Victor's back. Before Victor could knock him off, he upended the flask of holy water all over Victor.

"I rebuke you in the name of Jesus Christ, the son of God, Child of the Holy Virgin," William said. Once again the words felt like mud in his mouth. Once again, nothing happened. He was certain, however, that he'd pronounced the right invocation for divine assistance.

Victor flung William away again, and he sailed over the dining table, knocking down several chairs on his way down to the floor. Bruised and bleeding from his cheek, William got to his feet again. He stared at Victor, then at the empty flask on the floor, confusion clearly etched on his face.

Victor too stared at the empty flask, quickly understanding that William's holy water had failed to kill him. He sneered at William, "Your holiness is in doubt, father."

William gazed helplessly at Kate. Victor too turned to look at Kate, smiling when she flinched, then turned back to William again. "Is *she* the matter, priest? Too many sins of the flesh?" He laughed out loud: "I sense dirt on you, priest. Lust, the cardinal sin of the flesh: a filthy cloak dulling the grace of the hated almighty."

William grimaced. Now he understood why the water hadn't worked on the vampire woman downstairs. *I am the problem. I'm too far from God. I am not holy any more, like a priest should be.* Wincing, William remembered the semen stain on his cassock, and how he'd fucked Kate whilst he was wearing the priestly garment. If that wasn't a slap in the face of the Almighty, he didn't know what was.

I'm sorry, Lord he thought desperately. *I accept and understand my faults, and I repent. Please strengthen me like you did Samson against the Philistines after he was captured and blinded. Strengthen me to kill this enemy.*

In repentance, William found strength of a sort: a feeling that God was less angered with him than previously. He looked around desperately for a way to save Kate and himself, too far from either a stake or a cross. He was glad Kate wasn't rushing to attack

Victor from behind, now the vampire had his back to her.

Victor advanced on William. His horrible eyes gleamed with the assurance of victory. Stalking forward, he seemed to grow in stature.

"Now you will die!" he screamed at William, rushing at him.

Then William saw the light. Literally. A single spot of sunlight on the dining room wall, created by a stubborn sliver of sunshine, had somehow penetrated the enshrouding curtains.

William wondered how he'd overlooked the obvious: Vampires couldn't face daylight!

In a flash, he leapt to the window and pulled back the drapes. Immediately as the sunlight poured into the room, Victor halted in his tracks. He raised a hand to cover his face. His hair caught fire.

"It's working!" William yelled at Kate, "Help me get the other drapes open."

Kate had, in the meantime, extricated herself from her nook of partial safety between fridge and crockery cabinet. She didn't move toward the window, however. Instead, she stood in front of the huge fridge, looking at the burning vampire with what seemed like regret in her eyes.

Oh, hell, William thought, but shouted, "Do it, Kate!"

Victor's entire body was smoking now, wisps of black vapor peeling off his skin. He looked like he'd burst into flame at any moment. He searched the room with desperate eyes, eyes full of the knowledge that he was about to die, eyes full of the horror of the daylight.

"Go to hell, you murdering bastard!" William yelled. "This is for my cousin!"

Victor turned towards Kate, and William watched him rush at her, a sinking feeling in the pit of his stomach. *Oh, hell, what have I done now?* He sprang after the vampire, trying to stop the inevitable.

Fearful expressions spread over Kate's face as Victor approached her. However, the smoking vampire – his face a mask of terror – wasn't interested in Kate in the least. He knocked her roughly aside and pulled the fridge doors open. Inside the fridge was a female body suspended on a meat hook, which Victor yanked off the hook and flung out of the fridge and away. Then he leapt into the fridge and pulled the doors shut on himself, escaping the daylight.

William and Kate both stood speechless, staring at the giant refrigerator with its undead captive. William rushed over to her, taking her in his arms, "Are you okay, darling?"

She nodded back, shivering, but getting a hold on herself, "I'm fine. I'm sorry, I just switched off right now."

"Did you find the kid?" William asked her.

Kate shook her head, "No. He isn't anywhere in the house. No cradle or any baby things either."

William nodded sadly, "The bastard. A little child? You killed a little child?"

The dining room was now flooded with sunlight, everything outlined in stark contrast.

Kate nodded at the fridge, "He's trapped in there for good."

William shook his head. "Only until nightfall. He'll be super strong then, so we've got to finish him off long before that."

He turned and studied the corpse Victor had thrown out of the fridge. The body was a young redhead, early-to-mid teens, with a heavily freckled face. Her bodice was ripped open, the entire top half of her pubescent breasts gnawed and clawed to shreds. Her throat . . . William looked away from the corpse in disgust.

Time to finish this monster off.

He tramped angrily off and picked up a cross from the floor, then located and picked up his own cross also. He fiercely jerked the stake out of the dead mercenary's chest and returned to Kate's side.

He handed both crosses to Kate. "He can't come out," he whispered harshly. "Once I get the door open, throw one cross inside.

Kate moved out of the way and William heard her fiddling about behind him. He prayed she wouldn't freak out on this, or wasn't getting out her digital camera like a fan so she could photograph the vampire's end. He shrugged. *Doesn't matter. Once I get this door open, Victor is toast. Fry, you godforsaken bloodsucker!*

William grabbed the fridge's left door with his left hand, holding the cross tightly in his right hand. Expecting Victor to be wrenching the fridge door shut from the inside, he braced his foot against the foot of the fridge.

In deep concentration, he mentally rehearsed his actions: *Jerk the door open fast, stab inside and upward, once . . . twice . . . thrice. The cross Kate will throw inside will disorient him enough for me to get the stake deep into his black heart.* He decided he was ready.

"Okay, baby," he told Kate, "Let's do this."

"I'm sorry, baby," Kate said, "but I can't let you do that."

"Huh?" William turned around. He stared in incomprehension at the taser Kate was holding. He was even more uncomprehending when she tasered him with it. Like vampire teeth, both the taser's wires stabbed William in his neck, and the electricity pulse kicked into William's muscles. He dropped his stake and began to spasm; body jerking like he was having a seizure, William crashed to the ground and landed on his side. Twitching, and with no idea what was going on, he watched Kate, still wearing her moviegoer smile, bend down towards him.

Where the hell did she find handcuffs? he wondered, paralyzed and unable to protest, as she locked his wrists together. Then she got out another set of handcuffs and clipped together his ankles. With William still staring at her dumbfounded, Kate got out her cell phone and made a call.

"Hey, Joey. Yeah, it's done, so bring the boys over. No, it didn't go according to plan. Tarrant and all his men are dead... How? We had some good luck. Bring a truck over, the vampire's stuck in this huge fridge and we need to move it."

161

CHAPTER 17

Kate was glad now the masquerade was over and she could be her calm efficient self again. She looked down at William. The shock was wearing off, and he looked enraged.

"What are you fucking doing?"

She smiled coldly, "Calm down, darling. What does it look like? We just caught us a live vampire. Victor Rothenstein, no less!" Again, that Southern accent.

"What?" He looked at the fridge, then back at Kate. "Then everything...?"

Kate smiled at William's bemused expression, "Yes *darling*, everything was a setup to get you to work with us to catch Victor."

"Even our relationship?"

Her smile saddened, "Yes, even that. It was imperative that you work with us on this."

"Us? Who? The U.S. government?"

Kate grinned back, but said nothing. *William is so naive,* she thought. She was saddened that she'd hurt him, however. She'd not expected to enjoy seducing him so much. It was his innocence that did it – his simplicity, the way everything was always new with him, over and over again. She'd liked him from the start, and that had grown into...

But then, everything must come to an end, she thought.

Joe's mercenaries entered then: six cold-faced men who gave Kate the shudders. Each of them had been handpicked by Tarrant for this assignment, and well paid – a million dollars each in a numbered off-shore account. All had seen combat, and were part of the best the US Army had once had to offer. None had any scruples – they were very well prepared to commit murder if need be.

Joe walked over to Kate. He was tall, with a broken nose, and a blond crew cut. He'd been Tarrant's Lieutenant in the gulf.

"What happened to Martin?" he demanded of Kate.

She stared coolly back at him. "Not entirely certain. They're downstairs in the basement. Take some of your men and investigate."

"Take stakes and hammers too," William said, overcoming his disgust with the situation. "Stake anyone who still has a head, through the heart. Else they'll turn into vampires too."

Joe looked at Kate for approval.

"Yeah," she said, dismissively. "Do as he says – he's the expert. Stake 'em all. Tarrant too – if he's still got a head."

Joe nodded curtly. He called two men to follow him and the trio departed from the living room.

Kate turned to the remaining five men, and tapped the fridge. "He's in here. We ship him before nightfall. Is the plane ready?"

One of the men nodded.

"Okay, who's got the silver wire?" Kate snapped, and a mercenary stepped forward with a reel of wire wound on a large red spool. "Bind the fridge and let's go."

Two men moved to the fridge. One switched it off at the wall, and disconnected the socket. Then they pushed it forward and William watched the mercenaries loop coils of silver wire repeatedly around the fridge.

"You really came prepared for this," William said, disgustedly.

Kate looked at him. "We've been planning it a long time. Taking note of just about every eventuality. Nice that it worked out."

"What if it hadn't? It almost didn't. We could all be dead now!"

"True – but it did. Why bother with what might have been?" She smiled at him, "We've you to thank for that. Recruiting you was our master-stroke."

William winced.

Kate added: "You were right: theorizing about vampires is an entirely different thing from encountering them in person."

A mercenary entered then, rolling a massive hand truck before him. The other four mercenaries manhandled the fridge onto the truck and strapped it in place, then they rolled it out of the room.

Kate left William and walked after the men, to wait at the basement stairwell door. Joe and his men came up shortly. He looked shaken. Kate looked at him inquiringly.

"All done," Joe said. "Damn. I've seen some things in my time, but nothing like the scene in that basement. "

"You staked 'em all? Remember what the priest said."

Joe nodded wearily. "We stripped off their flak jackets and did them each through the heart. Shame 'bout Tarrant, though." He looked into the dining room, at the space where the fridge had been, observing, "I see you've moved our target." He then pointed to William, who'd now managed to stand up. "What do we do with the priest?"

Kate thought a moment. "Bring him along. He knows too much, and he's a do-gooding sort of guy. Might talk to all the wrong people."

"Killing him will solve that, too," Joe said. But Kate shook her head emphatically. Joe shrugged, then signaled the other two men who strode into the room.

"Don't make a fuss, darling!" Kate called through to William. "We wouldn't want to *have* to kill you."

William didn't make a fuss. The mercenaries picked him up between them and carried him out of the room.

A large moving truck was parked in the driveway. As the group assembled near the rear of the truck and prepared to load the refrigerator, several shots rang out – bullets heading in their direction.

"Youse ain't stealing the damn sausage freezer, ya crooks!"

It was Marv. The hired hand was shooting at the group from within the pig stall with a .22 caliber pistol. This was used sometimes for shooting pigs and varmints, and Marv found it whilst rummaging around the office. One of the bullets managed to hit the refrigerator, chipping a small hole in the door. A hissing sound could be heard from inside.

"Quick, Joe – duct tape the hole so our prize doesn't burn up!" Kate barked.

She shoved William down behind the refrigerator to keep him from getting shot. William was not expecting this and fell, hitting his head on the refrigerator, knocking him unconscious.

"And you!" she shouted to another soldier. "Take care of that fucking retard!"

The mercenaries quickly took cover behind the refrigerator and the moving van and efficiently returned fire. Their bullets killed Marv instantly.

"Let's get out of here!" Kate announced.

William didn't remember much of the ride to the airport or the plane trip afterwards. The plane itself was a huge cargo carrier parked on a deserted corner of the Youngstown-Warren Regional Airport. Still bound hand and foot, William was carried up the loading ramp by the mercenaries and dropped on a seat beside the refrigerator that housed Victor.

"Where the hell are we going, Kate?" he asked her as she sat opposite him.

She smiled. "Your old home – Melas."

William gaped back at her in horror. He stared at the fridge containing the vampire and his horror doubled. He had no idea what was going on, but he did know that whatever it was, was very bad.

Kate blew William a kiss. "Stop looking so worried, baby. This will all turn out well for you. Just relax and enjoy the flight."

The cargo plane taxied down the runway and lifted into the sky.

PART 3

STOLEN SOUL HOUSE

CHAPTER 18

Jackie Nixon stood with her hands on her hips, perusing the freestanding three-dimensional model of Melas, nodding as the architects and engineers explained progress, pointing out new features, explaining that they were keeping to the integrity of the old town but ensuring a modern, contemporary feel and facilities appropriate to the twenty-first century.

All Jackie heard was 'blah, blah, blah.'

The only plans she was truly interested in were the ones enabling the rebuilding of the old Madison House. And she kept a very careful eye on those. She demanded that Donovan Smith brief her regularly – and then literally de-briefed her, as she insisted on stripping off her panties and their making love at every opportunity. After all, she needed to keep him on board, as well as satisfying her own physical needs: as basic as they were. She held no truck with loving looks and gentle sweet nothings whispered in ears. She couldn't be bothered with courtship, extended foreplay, seduction, adventurous or even different positions, role-play or anything that wasn't straightforward, functional sex. Don fulfilled a purpose for her, like comfort-eating a hamburger when you're hungry: basic, uncomplicated working fare that meets a need.

Also, while he kept having sex with her, Jackie had something over him. He was terrified that Alison would find out, but compelled to continue their affair. For one thing, Mike kept warning him to keep their employer sweet; for another, if he didn't please Jackie, he feared not only for their work and the massive profit it would reap, but for his marriage, too. Jackie was a powerful woman. He wouldn't like to cross her. He was even more terrified since her billionaire husband George had recently died of a heart attack at the age of seventy-three. If he wasn't much of a threat before, he was a far greater threat now that he was dead. Jackie Nixon was a staggeringly rich widow: a single woman. What if she wanted more from Don? He worried things might get serious.

Don had been hoping to keep the re-build of the old Madison House on the low-down. Sure, people would find out soon enough by seeing the site construction, but he certainly didn't want people to know about the bizarre and eccentric requests Jackie had made to incorporate the sand, clay and tar sludge from the bottom of the lake bed.

Don's initial appalled response had dulled as time went on. First, he gave her chances to change her mind, "But Jackie – we can get you the finest quality sand. Fuckin' diamond dust if you want it. You can afford it! That sand's contaminated after the tar fires and the disaster – the graves were flushed out, for Christ's sake. The sand's probably full of ash and burnt bone at the bottom of that lake!"

Jackie stared at him, coolly. "It's a tribute to those that died, Don. What better memorial to the past than they become part of the future?"

Don shook his head, knowing that his arguments fell on deaf ears. What Jackie wanted, Jackie got. She wanted secrecy as far as was possible, so he provided it. Independent contractors had dredged the lake bottom, taking the sediment from the slurry; other contractors had processed, separated and dried it; another team had delivered it to the site, so the builders had no idea of its strange provenance when they mixed up the concrete and mortar and stacked the bricks. It was all sand and clay and normal building materials to them. Same old, same old.

Except for the fact that Jackie's eccentricities hadn't been limited to using the sand and clay from the lake bottom. Once the foundations were laid, she wanted more. She had a huge collection of stones: substantial smooth and shiny pebbles that she wanted incorporate into the walls, so the architect and masons were required to design and build them into the structure. She had also had people gather small chunks of shattered marble from further down Raccoon Run Road, from the yard of Walter Pinkman's house, which of course, she now owned too, since she had bought the entire town. She wanted these nuggets of marble also incorporated into the fabric of the Madison House.

"Oh," said one of the interior designers on an early site visit, waving a hand dismissively when the chief bricklayer queried Jackie's choices and questioned her taste, "It is an established artistic genre to incorporate 'found objects' in artwork. You're lucky the artist

Marcel Duchamp isn't involved, or you'd be making the house out of porcelain urinals!"

"What kind of crazy is that?" said the builder, scratching his head under his hard hat. "Make sure that guy doesn't set foot here!"

"It's OK – he died nearly fifty years ago," the designer smirked.

"Good," said the guy, squinting into the sun. "Well, I suppose with people like that in the world, maybe Mrs. Nixon's not so crazy after all…"

Alison Smith had eventually had to broach the subject of the rebuilding of the Madison House with her husband, since Don had not mentioned it at all. Meanwhile, she had sensed the spirit of Lucy Westerna looming over her in the background, as if breathing down her neck to remind her of her task to dissuade him from rebuilding the house. Alison waited for him to mention his new job, to no avail. She had dropped hints and made idle, oblique enquiries about the sorts of buildings that were being reconstructed in Melas, but eventually, after a day, she had to come right out and say it. She practically had to beg Don to tell her about the Madison House.

With Lucy Westerna's warnings ringing in her ears, Alison had been horrified when Don eventually confessed that he had been contracted to rebuild the old place, and had agreed on terms and a start date.

"Don – I don't want you to do it!" she cried, wide-eyed in fear.

"Al, what are you talking about? It's just a job!" Don was amazed by her reaction.

Alison bit her lip, not knowing where to start. How could she tell him that a ghost had told her that a terrible evil would be unleashed if the house was completed, and that their lives would be in danger? Worse, that the whole of creation was in danger! It was crazy! Only a few weeks ago, she would have been the first one to doubt the sanity of anyone purporting to hear or see ghosts.

"I... just have a bad feeling..." Alison said weakly. "I've... um... read something about the place being cursed."

A chill of unease flooded Don's body. He'd had a bad feeling too, when Jackie had first asked him to use the mud at the bottom of the lake. It seemed a weird and sinister demand, but she'd seemed earnest enough about wanting to honor the dead and to keep things local by using materials from old Melas. So he shrugged off the chill that Alison's words had elicited, and blustered, "That's not like you. Alison! Since when have you believed in that crap? I thought your book about superstition was going to de-bunk all that stuff!"

Alison's mouth opened and closed like a fish, trying to formulate an explanation, until she admitted, "I can't really explain, Don. You wouldn't believe me, because I can hardly believe it myself..." She stared into his concerned eyes, weighing up whether or not to tell him what had happened, but since she had no other way of telling him, she decided to be honest. "Okay," she gulped. "I'm not crazy, so don't start telling me I am, but... I saw a ghost. Really."

Don's eyebrows shot up to his hairline, and he almost laughed, before catching himself, seeing her pleading, slightly terrified look.

"I know, Don – you don't even have to say," she interrupted him before he could even respond. "I don't even believe in them, but there she was…"

"She?" Don asked, "What, like a white lady, a gray lady or something? Spooking you?"

"That's just the thing. She was dressed in contemporary clothes, and she was sad and serious, but otherwise, not really frightening – actually, quite friendly."

"Like Casper?" Don couldn't contain his urge to be facetious any longer, but he at least contained his rising laughter, straightening his face to listen, especially on seeing a flash of anger in his wife's eyes.

"I'm not joking, Don!" she exclaimed. "She told me her name – Lucy Westerna. I even checked her up in the Melas records, and she did live here – she died only a couple of years ago in a big old fire at the children's home…"

Don not only remembered hearing about the fire at the time, but he had cleared this very site for the Moran-Smith construction camp they were now staying on. He frowned. He knew his wife very well; knew she was an intelligent, sane woman who never lied but he couldn't conceive of what she was saying. It was too incredible.

"Al, I've said we'll do it now," he shrugged. "I'm bound by a contract. Besides, it's a special pet project of Jackie Nixon's. She's making it a home for her and George…" Since at that stage, George was still alive.

Alison's face dropped. So much so, that Don swallowed hard, feeling guilty. He wondered if all this fuss and fantasy was because Alison was envious of Jackie – jealous of him working for her. Or worse... did she know anything more? Don's forehead beaded with sweat as he scrutinized Alison's face for signs that she was aware of his betrayal, but Alison looked more panicked than upset, angry, or jealous.

"Don. You can't..." Alison said, her wild eyes begging him. "All I know is... if you rebuild that house – all hell will break loose!"

Don frowned, "Who with?"

"Evil," Alison whispered.

"Al... you're scaring me now," Don said, concerned. "Not because I'm afraid what you're saying is true – but because I'm worried about your mental state. Look, you've been working really hard on all this research... Shouldn't you take a..."

"Don! I'm not crazy," Alison said, grasping the sleeve of his shirt tightly, like a crazy person. "I know it sounds like it, but I am begging you now – the Madison House must not be rebuilt!"

Don stared into her eyes, still worried about her. "I have to," he shrugged. "I'm obliged. It was all part of the deal."

The deal with the devil, whispered the spirit of Lucy Westerna, audible to Alison. She spun round in her seat, her wide eyes searching for the figure of Lucy's ghost, but there was nothing there.

"What?" asked Don in alarm, more concerned than ever.

"Shhh!" hissed Alison, her ears straining to hear more. She was desperate for help or advice – a way of persuading Don not to take up this job. Because what Lucy had told her about the horrors that would be unleashed had turned her bones to water.

But there was no one to help.

CHAPTER 19

Forty years earlier, Walter Pinkman and his five year old daughter, Lyn, had moved to Melas, after the death of his beloved wife, Irene. Irene had been a really warm, loving mother who had protected her daughter somewhat from her husband's esoteric interests and beliefs, allowing Lyn to play and simply be a child. Walter spent most of his time in his office, poring over ancient texts, or traveling the world collecting arcane specimens and instruments of ritual magic.

Walter was the somewhat eccentric professor who emerged blinking from his office only for meals, whom Lyn saw rarely, but loved, nonetheless. But now that Walter was all she had, the little girl clung to him and idolized him more than ever. Walter had never been much good at baby talk or playing with toys with kids, even when he was a boy himself. He had always been intelligent and serious, and he certainly didn't believe in talking down to kids and patronizing them. Indeed, for him, his interests were as much fun as playthings. He delighted in his occult tomes, in discovering spells and rites, and practicing the ancient rituals he had learnt.

Indeed, he was on the edge of an amazing discovery when Irene died, and his excitement was equal to, if not exceeding his grief. So being landed with the full time care of a five-year-old girl was not going to stop his progress at this thrilling time.

Walter had been exploring the topography and geomancy of magic – how energy from the natural landscape can be harnessed for good or evil. Through his research, he learned that the geographical layout of the West Virginia hills actually channeled evil – drawing it like a magnet. In fact, West Virginia led the entire country in having one of the highest suicide rates and a disproportionate number of the population diagnosed with clinical depression. Health experts attributed this depression to a 'mountain culture' – whereby the populace experienced depression as a result of isolation from the rest of the outside world – cut off by the mountains and hills. Walter Pinkman didn't buy this theory at all.

Pinkman knew that the depression was due to a veil of evil that blanketed the land, and was simply more intense and darker in some places than others. Melas was such a place. Walter believed that Hell itself leaked out into the normal world in such areas, bleeding out its poison much like a cancer. Anyone who lived in these 'fringe' areas either died from the evil, experienced unprecedented hardships, or embraced the evil and found enlightened power from the dark forces. Walter would embrace it.

He hadn't been too sure how Irene would take his wanting to move to Melas, but fortunately, she had died before he had to broach the subject in all seriousness. Now, he was free to pack up his belongings – including his daughter – and live right in Melas to conduct the most practical elements of his theoretical research. He could take his necromancy to new levels using the power of the evil that simmered beneath the surface in Melas. His mind was buzzing with possibilities, and he didn't want to be distracted by taking time out and having to play with a five year old. If he couldn't adjust his regime to fit in with Lyn's, she would just have to conform to his way of life.

Unwilling to hire a nanny or a babysitter, because he didn't want people snooping around the house while he was conducting such groundbreaking occult research, Walter decided that he would include his daughter in his work and teach Lyn all she needed to know. She would become his little apprentice.

And so, they landed in Melas, to live in the house that would soon become known simply as Walter Pinkman's house, on Raccoon Run Road, within sight of the imposing Madison House.

"Why did we move, Daddy?" asked little Lyn, once all the boxes had been unloaded and unpacked and they had time to sit and breathe.

"Darling, this is a very special place," smiled Walter kindly. "Can you not feel the energies?"

The little girl rolled her eyes around the room, waiting to feel something. "Nope," she answered at last.

"Okay, maybe I should tell you a story that might help," said Walter, not entirely unaware of how to behave with small children. "Are you sitting comfortably?" The little girl nodded vigorously, her blonde ponytail thrashing up and down. "Then I shall begin. Once upon a time, the devil walked upon the land hereabouts...."

"The devil?" interrupted Lyn. "What's that?" For her kindly mother had mentioned God, but was not the sort of person to terrify her baby with mention of the devil.

"Oh, a very clever being," smiled Walter. "Not a man. A powerful being. More of a god."

"God?" Lynn scrunched up her nose. "God I pray to with mama?"

"Kind of..." Walter's smile faded a little. "But anyway. Back to the devil. Although he once lived in heaven – which mama probably told you about – the devil got thrown out, to a place called Hell."

"Thrown out?" Lyn remembered times when she'd thrown her teddies out of her cot, when she was young and foolish. "Who threw him out?"

"God," said Walter. "The one you call God, anyway."

"Naughty God!" Lyn squealed, because her parents called her naughty when she flung her toys in a rage.

Walter beamed, "That's right! Naughty God. Clever girl!"

It was Lyn's turn to beam, delighted with his praise. She liked her father to think she was clever. She wanted him to love her. And he clearly loved her and was very pleased when she listened to him and was clever.

Lyn had grown up and studied hard at her father's knee for many years until she knew as much as he did.

But, being home-schooled and not receiving the stimulus of other young people, she began to grow resentful. She had never learned to play with children, but she couldn't help noticing that she was different from the other kids she saw on her way to the store, or passing by the house.

Walter Pinkman's life's work had moved on apace since he had moved to Melas.

"Lyn, we are on the brink of something so exciting that it will change the world!" Walter said, his eyes blazing with excitement.

Initially, Lyn was thrilled too, infected with his excitement and passion. But although her father was progressing with his knowledge, harnessing the evil energies that lurked within the earth beneath Melas, the full potential he believed was possible always eluded him. It seemed to Lyn that he was always on the brink of something, and never actually getting there.

They didn't even have proper family dinners. Their dining room in the house was devoted to the ceremonies of ritual magick: rams' skulls and candles decorating the mantelpiece and the heavy dark oak table pushed to one end to act as an altar. A pentagram was first chalked on the floor, for use during their early experiments, and later painstakingly painted on the varnished wooden boards to offer a permanent fixture. Years later, after his successes, Walter would hastily paint over the whole floor to obscure this sign, but when Lyn lived there, they only had themselves to please.

When Lyn was twelve, she had fussed and nagged at her father to buy a television. Realizing that he hadn't given her much in the world apart from his undivided time – and even then, only as long as it suited his work – he relented, and Lyn came to know that she was missing one hell of a lot in terms of fashion, music, boys and worldly knowledge – although her other-worldly knowledge was far better than most.

And in that way that teenagers have – full of the arrogance of youth, she believed that she knew better than her father, and far more than he did. She became itchy to be out in the world. She eventually outgrew Melas and the claustrophobia of the Pinkman house, having only her father to talk to. Even then, his only topics of conversation were his esoteric studies and occult knowledge – and the beginnings of their experimentation on bringing souls back from the dead.

Once again, in the hushed darkness of the dining room, the heavy velvet drapes closed from prying eyes, Lyn and her father proceeded with the latest ritual. They were both robed in their scarlet ceremonial robes, her father's features set stone-like in concentration as he held the *athame* aloft. This was the ceremonial dagger he used, which he had purchased from a pagan dealer in Wales, Britain, who reckoned it was pre-Druid and had powers to call back souls from the Underworld.

"All the elements are coming together, Lyn!" he grinned, almost crazed with delight, as he'd ripped open the box with the overseas postage seal on it. He quickly tore the plastic wrap from around the athame, and gasped.

To Lyn, it looked like a rusty old hunting knife, but if it pleased her dad – well, it was his money.

"Lyn – with this, accompanied by the powers of Melas itself, we are going to be closer than we have ever been to resurrecting a soul!"

Yeah. Sure. We always are, thought the fourteen year old Lyn, growing more cynical and impatient as the months passed.

So here they were again, all robed up with no place to go. Lyn had smudged the altar with sage and sweetgrass and they had arranged the candles in order on the altar in a slight curve: black, blue, green, white, green, blue, black. Heady incense burned in front of the white candle, with a human skull placed behind the incense.

The pair meditated in silence before the altar as the wisps of smoke from the incense settled. Then Walter lit the candles one by one from end to end, the flames flickering excitedly as if mirroring Walter's expectation.

He carefully placed a number of stones in front of and around the skull and incense.

Then he chanted: *"Cerberus, curator of silenti, sino phasmatis venire contra mihi."* He turned, and raised his hands, intoning: *"Phasmatis, radix quod causa of vita, commodo adeo suffragium mihi in meus negotium."*

Her father fell silent and bowed his head. Lyn knew that they had to meditate until they felt spirits around them. Lyn stood, feeling nothing again. Until... beyond her wildest dreams, she felt a strange tingling she initially thought was her imagination, but then, through a haze of wonder and disbelief, she realized that her father must feel it too, because he moved onto the next phase of the summoning, calling out: *"Gratias ago vos Cerberus, pro tabellae silenti etc transeo. Gratias ago vos phasmatis pro iunctio mihi in meus nisus."*

The air crackled with anticipation like electricity, and Lyn held her breath, trembling despite herself. Wasn't this what they wanted, after all? Wasn't this what they had spent years exploring?

But there were no thunderbolts or lightning strikes. No massive windstorms. No howling of gales, or of disembodied souls. No hell's mouth gaping open to allow tortured souls to rise. They waited for several minutes, eyes closed, breath shallow and barely discernible, but the odd thrilling feeling reduced and disappeared and nothing happened.

She opened her eyes, and waited, while her father stood there, his eyes still squeezed shut like a child at Christmas hoping for the gift he'd always wanted. Eventually he opened his eyes and dropped his hands, disappointed, and they slowly snuffed out the candles and cleared the things away again.

"We were so close, Lyn! So close!" her father chattered, "Next time, the soul stones are certain to be filled…"

Lyn stopped listening as she picked off spatters of wax from the table-top.

The teenage Lyn Pinkman felt like a dead soul herself. Sulky and depressed, she wanted something more from life than this. She had spent so much time exploring the realms of death and hell with her intense father beside her constantly that she was sick to the stomach. She wanted to be young and to feel alive!

More months passed, with her father's experiments and incantations coming to nothing, and Lyn's increasing frustration and cabin-fever eating away at her. She had to turn her mind to the outside world.

She investigated her own escape route and was on her way. When she was sixteen, sharply intelligent, determined and self-motivated, she completed her entrance exams well in advance of her years and won a scholarship to Brown to study Business. She left for Providence with barely a second's thought and never looked back.

Because she was pretty, blonde and slim, she attracted some attention wherever she went, but first had no idea how to handle it, resorting to aloofness and hostility. TV had given the young, impressionable Lyn her only insight into contemporary life. From the darkness of news coverage, she had learned all she knew about society, and from crime documentaries and soap operas she had learned all she knew of the workings of the human mind. Love and emotion were alien to her, although she had carefully observed people on TV, mimicked their facial expressions and friendly conversations, and learned to 'pass' as a normal young woman with some sense of empathy and humanity. But she had been careful not to become fully distracted by them.

She found it useful that she could detach from the emotional fray that others seemed to suffer. She also found it easier to manipulate people and take an objective, scientific view of relationships and events to achieve her aims.

She'd got the hell out of Melas, left for the university in Rhode Island, later settling in Houston, Texas, and living a new life of her own. She still telephoned her dad and received updates on his exciting new developments, which never amounted to much.

But after around fifty years of dedicated work, Walter had rung her up in great excitement ten years ago. He had found an ally in the person who lived in the old Madison House, who, remarkably shared his passion, and this alliance seemed to be key to his success.

"I have done it! I have created true soul stones!" he gabbled. "You remember I told you about the souls of the dead I've summoned, but they never stayed for long? I have succeeded in confining them to the stones! Lyn, you should come and see!"

Lyn was doubtful. She had heard of so many of his successes before that she couldn't help but respond with a skeptical, "Really?"

As if to prove it, Walter detailed the process by which he had succeeded. And from what she knew of his work, it did seem feasible. It piqued her interest, and although she had been keeping her own passion for necromancy secret, even from her own father, she had still been practicing. In the comfort of her own lavish home in Texas, she experimented with creating soul stones herself. Her father even sent her some as gifts. She now had a great collection. But she had no desire to become embroiled again. She had her own successful life and independence.

"But this is just the beginning!" her father cried, and she shook her head, bemused that he could never be satisfied without the next big thing.

Around four years ago, Walter had told her he was on the brink of another new exciting development. At the end of the telephone, Lyn habitually rolled her eyes. Walter told her he was experimenting with summoning up damned souls incarnate. That is, he was bringing up the damned, bodily. Not satisfied by the wispy figures and energy of Auntie Marj or Chief Running Deer, and the intangible forms he had connected with before and managed to pin down into soul stones, he and his pal Victor Rothenstein had been concentrating on summoning up demons and evil spirits. *That should take them another fifty years to achieve,* Lyn thought, with a smirk.

Walter told her every detail of the processes, spells, equipment and rituals, and it took her right back to the times she had spent with him, from the ages of five to sixteen, and the interest he had engendered in her that she had spent the rest of her life trying to resist. This huge task warranted some kind of marble monument – an obelisk – over the vortex to Hell that they'd placed in the grounds of the house. They had managed to contain many souls within the large structure, creating a single massive soul stone. Despite Walter's invitations and requests, Lyn still wasn't tempted to come back and celebrate with him, although her father had kept her up to date with all his developments until the day he died.

She never came back to Melas.

Until she married George, that is.

By which time, everyone had forgotten that old Walter Pinkman had ever had a daughter called Lyn. Or to give her full name: Jaclyn.

Let alone that she was back, calling herself Jackie, buying up the entire town and grimly proceeding to take up her father's grisly work again for her own selfish and dastardly purposes.

Now that she owned Melas, Jackie was rebuilding the Madison house to a very particular plan. Without revealing the truth, she had persuaded the masons to build her collection of soul stones into the walls of the building, along with the sediment covering the surface of the Floyd Lake bed that contained the ash and ground, burnt bones of hundreds of inhabitants of Melas. She also wanted as many chunks of the shattered obelisk containing human souls as could be found, too. All were being incorporated into the Madison house.

She was rebuilding the house from human souls.

CHAPTER 20

No matter how much she complained and pleaded, Alison Smith could not convince Don to give up on the reconstruction of the old Madison House. In the end, she accepted that whatever was going to happen, however chilling, she would have to face it when it came to it.

Considering her past as a debunker of all things paranormal, she supposed she couldn't blame her husband for disbelieving her wild story of ghostly visitations and warnings. But on another level, she couldn't help but feel betrayed by Don. He should trust her enough to know that she didn't lie. As for her spirit ally, while Alison occasionally thought she felt the merest vibration of Lucy Westerna's spirit around her, sometimes when she was alone and mulling over her worries, she never saw her or heard her again. Alison was on her own.

Despite his wife's misgivings, Donovan Smith was not going to argue with his powerful employer and part-time lover, Jackie. So he proceeded with the construction of the house, tailored to Jackie's bizarre requests for using local mud, sand, pebbles and marble chunks as part of the fabric of the building. But he had no idea of the real reason behind her obsession to rebuild the old manor house.

Whilst Jackie had kept safe, if distant, tabs on her father's experiments and listened to his enthusiasm by phone over the years, she had taken it all with a grain of salt. Walter Pinkman had been 'very close' and 'on the brink' of success for all the time she had known him, after all.

But then, she had discovered incontrovertible proof. It was Jackie's husband's company that had installed the surveillance equipment for the Lunatic Asylum, and after the flood destroyed everything, they were contracted to fix the damaged equipment. When the repair crew found that the videos were intact and contained recordings of what had happened, Jackie Nixon had demanded a private viewing.

The standard story was that patients and staff had drowned in the floods. Not that they were victims of a zombie apocalypse. The disaster was political dynamite, which the governor was happy to keep under wraps, but for Jackie, what she saw had a far greater personal importance.

It was only when she saw the surveillance video of events in the old mental hospital that fateful day that she had the proof she needed to truly believe the truth of what her father had managed to achieve. Resurrection. Life after death. The raising of the dead. Her father may not have been there himself to see the full extent of his results, but his legacy lived on. Literally. His partner and associate, Victor, had evidently taken things further still. With her own eyes, on the video footage, she had seen that dead woman in the bright nightgown stand up and walk, as clear as day. And others – many others – albeit in various states of death and decomposition, had been walking as living dead. Now, she had reason to believe that it was all possible. And now, her obsession with rebuilding Melas, especially the Madison House, was the result of that faith.

She had nothing to lose, and everything to gain. Even more so, now that her diagnosis had been confirmed. There was no way she was going to be incapacitated by chemotherapy, losing her hair and her looks, blown up with steroids, in some vain attempt to steal some extra months or years to live a life of increasing age and degeneration. Why would she put herself through all that when she could have eternal life?

It was becoming harder to keep her cancer a secret, but Jackie managed to turn that to her own advantage. She claimed she intended to build a hospital in Melas – The Jaclyn Nixon Health Institute – specializing in research into a cure for cancer, which explained to some degree her drive for completing the project. It also gave people like Donovan Smith the impression that her rationale for rebuilding the town was purely out of vanity and a desire for immortality. They thought she wanted her name to live on. How little they knew! She wanted more than her name to live on, immortal. If it was possible, she feared old age more than she feared dying. And she was deathly scared of that.

And so, her plan was building speed. Melas was the place to harness the power, and the old Madison

House, so important to her father's ground-breaking work, was the vortex-point of all that energy. This was the place where she could live, happy ever after... forever.

At the time that Melas' mini-apocalypse occurred with the floods and disaster at the Lunatic Asylum, Jackie had received reports of what happened in her hometown – both the 'public' version and the rumors of the truth. She watched the media reactions with an interest that was way beyond the norm. In fact, before she received the evidence of the video footage, she had scrupulously scanned the local and regional news reports for any hint of what she suspected had gone down. She paid people to investigate the rumors she had heard, and the surveillance video had pretty much sealed the deal for her. Two days after the disaster, there was a bonus: she discovered a news report concerning a trucker being found dead, with his body completely drained of blood. Jackie had stopped dead in her tracks, her mind whirling.

Vampire!

This was extremely exciting. There was a survivor, after all!

Jackie immediately set things in play to find him. Because if there was anything that would completely secure her immortality – even better than the untried method of harvesting spirit energy from soul stones to use for herself – it was vampirism. The one tried and tested way to become immortal and retain – and even regenerate – one's earthly beauty – it was to join the elite legions of the damned that were vampires. After all, nobody ever saw an ugly vampire.

Jackie practically purred with delight. If a vampire was walking amidst them, she was just one step away from immortality. And she would achieve it in style. Her house of souls would merely give her extraordinary power and insurance. With everlasting life, youth and beauty, and thousands of souls at her disposal to fulfill her every command, there would be no end to what she could achieve. She could rule the world if she wanted.

All she had to do was track down the vampire who could make her life complete.

It was vitally important that Pinkman's and her own collection of soul stones – or spirit stones – containing the trapped souls of a thousand dead people, were incorporated into the house. Also, that the pieces of broken marble of the obelisk were gathered and used in the same way. She needed that life force kept in suspension to add to the energy of Melas itself. She recalled her father telling her, "You do realize that even if a soul stone were physically damaged, the spirits are still trapped. It takes a different kind of magic to free them."

She smiled. She had that different kind of magic now. With all she knew, all she had learned, and all that her father had told her, she could summon up the souls from those stones, and she had another thought. Possibly... and she had more work to do on this... if, by any chance, she didn't succeed in tracking down the lone vampire, she believed she should be able to utilize the soul stones by sucking out their life forces into a distillation of souls, to invest in her own body. Effectively, she could live as many lifetimes as the souls she extracted from the soul stones. And she was greedy for life.

Jackie was a necromancer, like her father, and he had taught her well; but she still had work to do if she was to take her father's success further. He might have raised spirits from the dead, but he hadn't managed to extend his own life. Necromancy wasn't all about raising the dead, though. Indeed, it was far easier to lay the living to rest.

Once her old billionaire husband George was of no more used to her; once she had secured Melas for her own, Jackie had killed him using her necromantic skills, opening a grave-door and forcing his soul through it.

With some pride and satisfaction, Jackie looked back and pondered upon the event, which had been one of the most invigorating hours of her life.

She had subtly placed everyday items in the four corners around George's study to create the makings of an altar of the four elements: a feather to represent wind, a glass of water, a humidor of cigars to represent fire, and a terracotta pot plant to represent earth. She had muttered the preliminary incantations, felt the thrilling sensations of the brooding darkness below the earth, awaiting her command, and then casually called George into the room – ostensibly to look at some plans for the Melas re-build.

The air was charged with electricity. In the center of the room, a grave-door stood open and waiting, invisible to the normal person's eye, but as clear as day to Jackie. Like a dull gray coffin lid propped halfway up from the floor, it opened onto a deep, dark and gaping hole into whirling infinity. The heat of hell was perceptible to her, but she trusted that George would not be able to see or feel any of the threats surrounding him. Until it was too late.

"George!"

When George entered the room, he was oblivious to the danger he was in.

"What is it, honey?" he asked, mildly.

Jackie grinned lazily at him, "Come have a look at the latest drawings for the mall!"

He chuckled as he ambled over, "You gals and your shopping!"

"Sexist pig," Jackie muttered under her breath, along with a few other arcane words that primed the grave door and the swirling vortex beneath. Visible to herself alone, the grave door pulsated with an eerie green light in the space between herself and her approaching husband.

George stepped further towards the center of the room, and Jackie's eyes blazed in anticipation, her smile frozen. *One more step!*

As his ridiculous cowboy boot hovered over the throbbing, glowing grave opening, George's own amused smile twisted into a grimace of pain and shock. He stared at Jackie momentarily, a strange expression on his face: a combination of desperation and pleading as he clutched his chest and crumpled to the floor, face first. The floor throbbed like a massive beating heart, and the whole room turned red. Jackie knew now that his soul was being forcibly sucked out of his body into the fiery hell below. The grave door closed with a slam over his body, momentarily obscured. But as George struggled, and the process of soul-extrusion continued, the grave door began to fade. George's thrashing limbs and trembling head becoming more visible through the increasingly transparent coffin lid. The red throbbing heartbeat stopped as the grave door gradually disappeared completely, until George simply lay still and quiet on the floor, and all signs of the grave door and the evil within it had gone.

Jackie stepped forward and tentatively peered over George's body for a moment, making sure the process was complete. With some effort, she heaved his bulk over so that he now lay on his back. But she wasn't concerned with his physical body. That was just a cumbersome shell. In the spot where he had been lying, on the expensive Persian rug, lay a slick polished stone with an oily iridescence to it. His soul stone.

"Now, George. Good to see you like this," smiled Jackie, picking up the stone and holding it up to the light, marveling at the pretty rainbow colors that emanated from the dark, glossy surface. "You're more use to me dead than alive, anyway!"

In everyone's opinion, George appeared to have succumbed to a heart attack. He was in his seventies, after all – and with a sexy, energetic wife thirty years his junior, they were only surprised he'd managed to live this long.

Realizing that vampires live forever, Jackie's plan was to become one. All she needed was a vampire to bite her to inject her with the gift of everlasting life. But this needed careful handling. A vampire had the power to suck her dry and kill her, or to pass on immortality with a single discreet bite. She either had to trust the vampire completely, or have someone standing over them with stakes and silver bullets to coerce them, on pain of their own death. She would choose the latter. She never did trust people, let alone vampires. But it was a wonder what money could do to build trust and loyalty, and she certainly had plenty of money to buy as much loyalty as she needed.

All that remained was to find the vampire. She knew she was looking for a man, and she suspected that regardless of what the man looked like now, his true identity would be that of Victor Rothenstein, her father's old associate. Walter Pinkman had never mentioned that Victor was a vampire in so many words, in his daughter's presence, but Jackie wasn't stupid. She knew that Victor relied on Walter to attend to his daily business – visiting the bank on his behalf, attending meetings as his proxy during the day. Yet, Victor was no housebound cripple, unable to move or do things for himself. He was very active and energetic in the evening – always after dark – traveling with Walter to various sites to conduct rituals, driving his monstrous classic car, and even physically installing the marble obelisk.

"Then what is that matter with him?" asked Jackie.

"Victor is simply a sufferer of extreme photosensitivity," Walter had explained to his daughter, "which makes daylight unbearable to his eyes. He also suffers from a rare skin condition called *erithropoietic porphyria* which means that any exposure at all to sunlight makes him instantly break out in painful blisters and lesions that require immediate hospitalization."

That was why Walter needed to help him out by day. Her father's matter-of-fact and detailed explanation of this fascinating man's condition had made it all seem so plausible to Jackie at the time, but the more she thought about it, the more suspicious she had become. Her father's experiments had been far more successful once he had met up with Victor Rothenstein – as if accelerated by some secret knowledge.

Through her contacts in her husband's security empire and surveillance camera business, and her team of 'associates,' Jackie was able to pull in lots of truck stop and traffic light surveillance video recordings, two of which showed the mysterious Jeff Abraham, who supposedly died in the mine, walking around alive and well, a number of days later.

All that now remained was to find him. With the aid of Kate, who was a hacker, conducting the preliminary research, and Martin Tarrant, the mercenary, and his men to provide the muscle, Jackie was confident that she was close to success. The icing on the cake was Kate's involvement with that young priest, William McConnellson III. He had defeated Victor Rothenstein before, and Kate had assured Jackie that the lad was so head over heels in love with her that he would do anything for her. Well, here was his chance.

And today, Tarrant had reported that all the elements were in place, ready for the strike to capture Victor Rothenstein in his lair.

Jackie looked at her Tag Heuer watch, raised her eyebrows, and then checked her cell phone. No messages. She just hadn't heard from them yet with an update, which concerned her slightly.

But she had every faith in Kate.

Still, it was about time.

PART 4

THE MOTHER OF DARKNESS

CHAPTER 21

William's vision was blurred when he first opened his eyes to find himself lying uncomfortably on his side, on a concrete floor, with a throbbing headache. He tried to cradle his aching head in his hands, but discovered that he couldn't move. He was restrained in some way. This inability to move, accompanied by the dull clinking of metal made him peer down at himself, only to realize that he was bound with chains around his feet and hands.

What the hell?

He struggled for a moment to recall what had happened, but looking around at the interior of a large, roughly plastered room in the half-light, the sight of the large fridge across the room in front of him reminded him. He painfully dug his elbow into the concrete and lifted himself up into a sitting position, wincing at the grinding into his bones and the chains' 'shucking' sound, loud to his ears in the silence.

The fridge was still wrapped around in thick silver wire. William remembered that just as silver bullets would stop a vampire in its tracks, silver wire or thread used against vampires meant that they couldn't break the bindings and escape. So, the intact wire knotted around the fridge indicated that Victor was still inside it.

William frowned, a pang of sharp pain shooting to the bump on his head. *There's a vampire in the fridge? For fuck's sake! I'm chained up in some cellar or storehouse with a vampire in a fridge?*

What was more – it was his old arch-enemy, Victor Rothenstein.

William glanced across at the door. Doubtlessly locked, he decided to take his chances on getting as much information as possible from Victor before they killed him. Or whatever they intended to do with either of them.

Pushing with his chained feet and hands and dragging his ass haltingly along the concrete floor towards the fridge, William made slow progress across the room until he sat, panting, right outside the fridge door. Eyes fearfully wide open in the dimming light of dusk, William glanced nervously towards the door, uncertain how loudly he could talk before arousing any attention from his captors. He held up his fisted hands and banged them against the fridge door, his chains ringing on the metal.

"Rothenstein!" he said as loudly as he dared, his mouth close to the rubber seal on the door in the hope that some sound would travel through it.

There was a muffled sound from within. William pressed his ear close.

"Is that you, *'priest'*?" The sarcasm was unmistakable, even through the thick door. The sound came from high up rather than through the door seal.

William lifted his eyes and spotted the taped 'X' where a bullet had pierced the shell of the fridge.

William struggled onto his knees to get closer to the sound. He had things to say, but more than that – he wanted to hear the vampire's answers to his questions. He raised the heavy chains on his wrists, and pulling on the handle, lifted himself to his feet with some difficulty, and began to pick at the edge of the tape with his fingernails, all the while talking as best he could in hushed tones.

"Yes – it's me, creep."

"Now, now," reproached Rothenstein. "After all, we could help one another out, here."

Bile rose in William's throat, "There's no way I'll help you, after you killed my whole family."

"Me?" Rothenstein mocked. "I heard they died in an accident. My condolences."

William swallowed the bile, shaking his head. "Look, I understand you killing Jonathan and Amanda for revenge, but why the hell did you kidnap the baby?"

There was a moment of silence, then a laugh of disbelief from within the fridge. "What are you talking about?"

William, having raised the edge of the tape, peeled it back fully. Now that the room was entirely dark, he saw only darkness within the fridge itself.

"You know what I mean!"

"I don't know what the hell you're talking about, priest."

William frowned, suddenly doubtful. What did Victor Rothenstein have to gain by denying it? He would get more pleasure from boasting about it. If he was the one responsible.

William's voice quavered uneasily, "Amanda's baby... It disappeared from the hospital the night of the accident. "

Another couple of seconds of silence passed while Rothenstein absorbed this information. Then, as if realization had suddenly hit him, he burst out laughing, his laughter rocking the whole fridge.

"Ahahahaha! AHAHAHAHA!"

Alison's husband Donovan had never believed his wife's hysterical demands that he abort his mission to rebuild the Madison House, of course. Partly because Jackie Nixon was so unbelievably rich, and his employer – he was being rewarded very well indeed with cash way beyond what the task warranted. Or possibly because he didn't want to rock the boat too much, because he was still fucking Jackie. She was beautiful and single, after all. She had confided that she had cancer, and it was slowly becoming common knowledge, especially with her wish to create a cancer center in her name. All of that simply added to Don's reluctance to upset her. In short, it was far easier to ignore his wife's concerns than to confront his rich, powerful, terminally ill mistress and potentially make an enemy of her. Worse still, she had the ability to destroy his business, his marriage and his life. Playing along with her eccentric design whims was the least of his problems within the context of everything. The house was nearly entirely built now; this particular job was almost finished, and then Alison would have to shut up and things could get back to normal again.

Unable to persuade Don to halt progress on the construction of the Madison House, Alison Smith had thrown herself into preparation for the worst possible scenario, when it seemed that she might have to take action, if nobody else would believe her. She needed to find out as much as she could about that old place, about the people who had lived there, and about all that was associated with the place. She had discovered a great deal from exploring Walter Pinkman's house and examining some of the books she'd found there. Enough to realize that she was dealing with some heavy duty shit, here. Her access to the university library, local history archives and the findings of her extensive research had led her to determine that there actually was something bad about the Madison House, even before Jackie Nixon had got her hands on it. A doctor called Henry Cane, his brother, Talman, and a certain Victor Rothenstein had a long history there, and their names recurred in the local history archives she had come across. Along with the information she had on Walter Pinkman's work, and her own decades of study and teaching in paranormal and esoteric areas, she built a sound foundation to prepare her for whatever would happen.

She was sitting in her home office, poring over some transcriptions of interviews with elderly residents of Melas from the nineteen eighties, when she felt a presence behind her, as if someone was leaning over her shoulder: someone with cool breath, the breeze of which made the hairs on the back of her neck stand on end. She turned around quickly, but there was nobody there. Yet, before she even heard anything, she strongly felt that the spirit of Lucy Westerna was with her again.

"They have a baby," a clear whisper said in Alison's ear. She recognized it as Lucy's voice.

"Who do?" Alison asked, frowning. "What baby?"

She swung around again, but still, there was no visible sign of Lucy's ghost. Only the spirit voice, and a definite coldness, as if an icy blast was hitting the side of her face as the whisper continued: "The vampires have kidnapped a human baby, which they intend to sacrifice when the time is right. And that time is... imminent. Tonight!"

Alison sat stock still, unable to speak; unable to conceive of what this meant, or what she could do to prevent it. As if Lucy's ghost read her mind, the whisper responded to her thoughts.

"If the baby is sacrificed it will open a door between this realm and that of the Darkness, where the vampires originate from. It will unleash all the powers of Hell upon the earth! You must stop it!" Lucy's disembodied whisper hissed intimately in Alison's ear.

"But how can I?" Alison exclaimed in horror. She was just one woman!

"You have sufficient arcane knowledge," Lucy murmured. "It is time to get it out of your head and into action. And you, yourself, are the only person who can deal with what is about to happen."

Alison swallowed down the bile rising in her throat. "But... I can't do it alone."

"There is only you. They hold the other one powerless. The priest. It is up to you alone."

"Will you be there, at least?"

She felt the air shift around her, and knew the answer before it was muttered. "No. I cannot. It takes someone alive in body and soul, passionate of heart and informed in mind. You, and you alone, are the one. Trust yourself. You know instinctively what to do."

Alison slowly shook her head in disbelief that it had come to this. A few months ago, she wouldn't have believed in ghosts, let alone listened to their advice. But at least she wasn't going crazy, hearing voices in her head. She could have so easily believed that she needed psychiatric care if she hadn't seen the spirit manifestation of Lucy for herself. No wonder Don had trouble believing her – no wonder he questioned her sanity! She hardly believed it herself! It was just a ghost, so she concluded that it was the lesser of the two evils of haunting and madness. But Lucy was a friendly ghost. This, apparently, was nothing compared with what she would have to face, very soon. Tonight.

Lucy's presence dissolved in the air, and Alison felt herself again completely alone. She looked down at the floor, vaguely seeing, but not really noticing, that the sheaf of papers she had been holding had dropped out of her hands at some point and lay scattered around her feet. She ignored them. She had other things on her mind.

She stood up, determined now, and strode across the room, crouching to pull out a locked heavy, long metal chest from under her deep shelving system. She lifted a thin chain from around her neck and took hold of the key that had been hanging from it, screwing it into the lock and opening the lid. She sighed heavily, gazing at the contents of the metal box. She had been collecting these things in earnest over the last few weeks in readiness. If she had to act alone, she would arm herself as best she could. One by one, Alison removed each item: her inventory of hope, placing them in a rucksack. An eight-inch wooden cross. A small mallet. A sharpened wooden stake. A bottle of holy water. A three-inch crucifix on a chain, which she hurriedly pulled over her head, where it lay heavy on her breastbone. Finally, from the bottom of the long chest, she withdrew a long object sheathed in leather, which she pulled off to reveal a polished silver short sword of two and a half feet long.

Its slim, sharp blade glittered dangerously.

She would fasten the sword belt around her waist when she got closer to her targets.

Pushing the sheathed sword diagonally into the rucksack and emphatically zipping it up before swinging it onto her back, Alison grimly headed for the Madison House.

CHAPTER 22

"**V**ery cozy!"

At the sound of the female voice behind him, and the electric light flooding the darkened room, William spun around from the refrigerator door so fast that the weight of his chains caused him to overbalance and crash awkwardly to the concrete floor. He gave a cry of pain as his elbow took the full force of his weight.

"What's happening?" Victor's muffled voice yelled from within the fridge.

Jackie Nixon stood with her hands on her hips, her head cocked curiously to one side.

"Having a chat? Making friends?" she said sarcastically. "Strange. I thought you two were sworn enemies. I would say 'mortal enemies,' but, well, Victor Rothenstein is immortal, isn't he?" she laughed bitterly.

Lying on the floor, struggling to get his body off his badly bruised arm, William gritted his teeth and stared venomously at this woman.

"So. You must be the 'boyfriend'."

Again, her harsh and mocking tone rattled William. Through his blurred vision, as he squinted to focus, he made out a slim blonde figure behind the older blonde woman speaking to him.

Kate! For a moment, his heart leapt with hope at the sight of her, until he remembered that she had been instrumental in his capture. Betrayed, he felt a stab within his heart.

"And '*boy*' friend is correct. Kate, you're practically a pedophile. What is he? Fourteen?"

Kate said nothing, her face impassive. And William was grateful for that. If Kate had started mocking him too, that really would have twisted the knife in his heart. He pushed himself into a sitting position, staring incredulously at Kate – the woman he loved. The woman he believed had loved him.

What the hell's going on here? he thought, his mind scrambling back to the intimacy of their love affair, and the sudden bizarre turn of recent events. He had been so absorbed in talking to Rothenstein over the last few minutes, he hadn't had a moment to ponder upon why Kate had betrayed him like this. He looked helplessly at her, his eyes pleading for an explanation, but she turned her pretty head away. *A little shamefaced*, he thought. She took a couple of steps back into the background, all her spark extinguished. She just wasn't his Kate at all now. What did this woman have over her?

"Awww…" the older woman began, in mock sympathy. "I can see you're confused, but I have no time for introductions and explanations. You've done as much as we wanted. You can be dispensed with soon. But first, I have more pressing matters to attend to," she smiled, staring voraciously at the fridge as if she could see the figure of Victor Rothenstein within.

She took a few steps forward and placed both of her hands outspread on the fridge door, her eyes wide and gleaming with a kind of lust.

"Rothenstein!" she breathed against the bullet hole in the door, speaking seductively. "Victor... may I call you? Since I hope we might become more... intimately acquainted."

Silence was the response. Within the fridge, Victor's brain was working overtime. *Who was this woman?* He had expected to be staked by somebody as soon as the door was opened, but this woman's wheedling tone suggested something different. He wasn't sure what, at this stage. *Sex? Collaboration?* And then, because he had been approached in such a way many times over the centuries, he knew.

"Yes, night has fallen now," Jackie mused, pressing herself against the fridge door, and still speaking breathily. "If I opened this door, you would be safe enough. But as it stands, you are still bound by silver wire."

"I know that, woman!" Rothenstein roared, finding his voice again. "Don't you think I would have let myself out before now?"

"Perhaps we can come to some sort of agreement... since I have the capability to assist you... or kill you."

William was torn between watching Jackie Nixon's seduction and threatening of Rothenstein, and trying to puzzle out what was going on with Kate. She, however, refused to meet his eye, staring determinedly at Jackie, as if literally watching her back. When William's eyes had completely adjusted to the light and he could focus, he noticed that Kate held a small silver pistol in her hand. It looked more of a decorative piece than a real weapon, but he was sure it could still do some damage if need be. Certainly, if she'd wanted to, she could have turned the gun against Jackie Nixon. Clearly, Kate was working for this woman, but was it under duress? What had happened for her to turn against him like this? Had she loved him at all? Was it all just a trick to lure him here, on the trail of Rothenstein? Just how calculating was Kate? Had she never loved him? His mind whirled.

One thing was for sure – he couldn't trust Kate at all now.

CHAPTER 23

Access to the grounds of the Madison House had been easy enough. Alison had previously made copies of the gate and house keys from Don's site office, and Don himself had told her that Jackie didn't want any security guards around the house site, only at the perimeter of the town itself.

The whole town was a construction site, so it made sense to hire a security company to protect the entire site rather than individual plots. Because Don ran the whole show, he and Alison had ready access, since they were still living in temporary accommodation on the site itself.

Alison simply had to make her way across the half-built town, and then she would unlock the perimeter security gates to the house, and probably the back door, she thought. Although she had no idea whether vampires would pre-cognitively know that she was on her way, or even care if she marched in through the front door. She would make up her mind when she saw the place, and checked out any lights or occupied rooms.

In the newly-planted undergrowth outside the freshly-built Madison House, Alison had already buckled up the sword belt, so the silver sword, in its scabbard, lay reassuringly against her thigh. She dispensed with the large rucksack now, and had placed the other items either in the open pockets of her cargo pants, or hanging from a tool belt she had wrapped diagonally across her body and over her shoulder like a gun holster. She had thought of everything – she hoped, at least.

There were no obvious lights switched on in the house: at least, none that she could see from this angle, but she intended to circle the house to check. Crouching over, she ran around the land in back of the house, keeping to the shadows of the specially-planted mature hedges Jackie had ordered the garden designer to buy at great expense. She was "too impatient to even wait for plants to grow," Don had laughed. But Alison was grateful of her extravagance at this moment. In her dark clothes against the bushy black-lit shrubs, she hoped she was invisible.

At the far end of the back yard, Alison stopped dead still and stared at the back of the house, her heart beating hard in her chest. There was a sliver of light emanating from the house at ground level – in the basement or cellar, presumably.

She swallowed hard and ran towards it, trusting that anyone in a brightly lit room would be unable to see a dark figure in the blackness outside. If she sprinted, she could take cover against the wall of the house itself, and then no one would see her, even if they looked out of the dark windows. Then she would try the back door – unlock it if need be – she had the key. And she would be inside, ready to face whoever or whatever was there. Ready to avert whatever cataclysmic disaster of a global scale was about to be unleashed.

Variations on Lucy's words were her mantra. If she felt herself falter, she came back to them: *I know what to do. I have the knowledge. I, and I alone, can stop this!*

It was true. Her years of studying the paranormal and parapsychology had so far been theoretical and academic. This was truly experiential field work, and it was time to put her learning to practical use. Now, she would discover, in a very harsh way, the difference between mythology and reality. Unfortunately, it would also prove the difference between life and death. But more than her own life was at stake now. She might be putting herself at risk in attempting to prevent a terrifying evil here today, but she knew that if she didn't try, she and millions of others would probably die in even more terrible ways, their souls infinitely suffering beyond death.

She had to stop it. Whatever was being planned and executed with the ritual killing of a baby would effectively result in the end of the world. But Alison had to get that out of her head to live in the present moment. She shook her head to shake off the implications. She had to concentrate on the immediate steps she needed to take to avert this disaster. If she thought of the results, it was all too much for her to handle.

Reaching the wall of the house, Alison stopped just next to the slit of the basement window at her feet. Breathing hard, she leant her shoulders against the stucco. Resting back, she was surprised to experience a sudden warm, soothing feeling, as if she was being embraced by warm arms. It was an extremely odd sensation, way beyond the relief of feeling safe from exposure and catching her breath.

It was as if the very fabric of the building was welcoming her.

CHAPTER 24

The blaze of light at ground level that had attracted Alison emanated from down inside the basement, where Jackie was still negotiating with the captive Victor. Although to her, the situation was non-negotiable. "So... let me propose a mutually beneficial arrangement," she said, "I will release you on condition that you... do a favor for me."

Although he could already guess what Jackie wanted of him, he kept silent for a moment, just to keep Jackie hanging in anticipation, and to give her a flicker of concern, before saying, "Go ahead. What do you want?"

Jackie licked her lips: "Your freedom, for... a taste of your blood."

William gasped. Even *he* knew that this not only meant immortality, but it was a far more powerful way of achieving it than by a vampire simply biting a human.

Vampires had the power to kill or to grant eternal life to a human, depending on the depth of bite and the amount of blood taken. They could drink their fill of blood for their own sustenance and drain a human dry, or mildly fang someone and give them immortality, primarily for companionship. Victor liked to call it 'the kiss of life'.

It was a lonely existence when you lived for hundreds of years amongst humans, outgrowing and outliving any of the rare human friends, lovers or companions that you made. You needed your own kind, too.

But in turn, some humans – wannabe vampires – would throw themselves at vampires, desperate to be fanged for the chance of eternal life. That was a risk: since the power was all in the bite, and therefore, all was at the vampire's discretion and whim.

Vampires ultimately made the choice of giving eternal life or death, and humans had little say in the matter when it came down to it. Victor had very rarely chosen to grant vampiric immortality to complete strangers who had requested it over the centuries. *He* was the one who had decided to fang each individual that had joined his small harem of vampire women to live with him at the farmhouse: not them.

Jackie's request to become immortal in itself was audacious, but he had expected it. What he hadn't expected was that she would ask to drink *his* blood. He had never permitted this in all his years of living death. Because giving a human his lifeblood meant giving away some of his own essence – and worse still, it would make her more powerful than himself. This was unthinkable.

However, he wasn't about to give up the opportunity to be released.

***

Unwillingly, Alison peeled herself away from the comfort of the wall outside the basement window, and immediately felt the cold determination that had brought her here in the first place. She unconsciously patted the sheathed sword at her thigh, and touched the mallet and cross hanging from her tool belt, as if reassuring herself by doing a brief inventory of the weapons she would need for her grim task.

She had no idea what she would find within the house. At the very least, she would probably come across Jackie Nixon preparing some kind of ritual. Possibly, her father's old pal Victor Rothenstein – the vampire himself. But she was prepared, and she had stealth and surprise on her side.

Clutching the small bundle of keys, she made her way soundlessly and swiftly towards the back door, her black sneakers softly brushing along the paving around the perimeter of the house. It was only a few yards, but it felt farther as she ran with her heart in her mouth.

She came to a stop and stood beside the frame of the glazed door, listening hard, but heard nothing, relieved that all was pitch black inside. Again, her body was only a fraction of an inch off that warm stucco wall, which felt so oddly relaxing and peaceful to lean against, but her target was inside.

Tentatively, she pressed the door handle, knowing that if it was locked, she had the key readily at hand. But to her surprise, the handle turned and the door opened easily, letting even more moonlight into the kitchen.

Alison followed it, stepping onto the marble flooring. She let her eyes adjust, but noticed that her fears had entirely left her. The same warming, attractive comfort as she had felt after leaning against the exterior wall consumed her, and she felt herself drawn further inside, across the expanse of the large, empty kitchen and into the dark hallway, where she saw a shaft of light pooling on the polished floorboards, indicating the open basement door.

Unable to stop herself, and with a somewhat other-worldly feeling of inevitability, she walked almost unconsciously towards the basement doorway.

As she approached, she heard the sound of voices. Or at least, a single female voice. The door was half-way open, so she didn't even need to touch it to slip inside, driven forward by that soothing warmth, which was stronger still inside the house.

As she peered inside, the first things she noticed was the strange interior decoration: the basement wall shone with the gleam of highly polished pebbles, inset into what looked like a black cement base. One step down, at the top of the staircase, she could clearly hear Jackie Nixon's voice now, and Alison paused, placing one hand on the basement wall to steady herself. Except, as if she had pressed against a flexible membrane, the wall gave way beneath her touch.

Alison felt herself lose her balance sideways, leaning in, but not finding anything solid beside her where the wall had been. It was as if the wall was melting like soft wax, and she was falling in slow motion into thick, semi-liquid blackness, which closed behind her and then held her immobile.

She tried to give a yell of alarm, but everything was surreal, like screaming in a nightmare, and no sound came out of her that she could hear. Instead, she could still hear Jackie Nixon's voice clearly enough; but far in the background, she also heard a low rumbling sound of many voices, like a crowd of hundreds, each in their own torment.

Not talking, but moaning softly, crying, and giving an occasional distant anguished scream, Alison tried to move, as if to swim through this thick atmosphere and back to the basement, but found that her movements were limited, and she couldn't. She was like a fly caught on flypaper, or suspended in aspic: an insect held in jello. And all around her, the distant background sound of haunting screeches and rumbling groans of other – *souls*, she thought.

This feels like hell! I am stuck here – literally in hell!

Trying to control her rising panic, Alison instinctively tried to turn her attention to the nearby human sounds in the real basement of the house, rather than the hellish sounds of captive souls god-knows-where. If she could stay conscious of the fact that she was only a foot away from the basement wall, wherever it was, she might keep a hold on reality – as far as she could make it out, and maybe she wouldn't get sucked into hell. Maybe she could still do something. Or at least, learn what the hell was happening. Maybe she could get back, if she fixed her attention on Jackie Nixon's voice. Because the sound was so close, it was as if she was in the room with her.

"What you ask has never been bestowed upon a human in my lifetime," came a man's voice. *Victor Rothenstein?*

CHAPTER 25

Unobserved by the other major players in the basement, William still sat on the ground, trying to work his bound wrists out of the tight chains, but it seemed hopeless. His ankles were tied, too: the ends of the chains held by padlocks. Without some kind of cutting gear – or the keys – he had no chance of escaping. Dripping with the sweat of his subtle exertion, he tossed his head to flick his drenched hair out of his face and suddenly caught Kate's eye. She looked quickly away.

Jackie was still speaking through the fridge door.

"So I'm your first. I love to be a pioneer," Jackie Nixon chuckled.

"Why should I do this for you, in particular?" Victor asked.

Jackie laughed mockingly. "Let me count the reasons... If you don't, you stay stuck in a refrigerator forever? Is that undignified enough for you?"

Victor Rothenstein wasn't even listening to her response. He was already calculating his next movements. Once this fucking door was open, he would fucking kill everyone in the place.

"Next – we kill you, unless you comply," Jackie added.

Yeah. Right, Victor smiled to himself inside the fridge. *Wait. Who is 'we'? The priest?* How many of them were out there? He started planning anew – how to take out a number of people. Although the sense he had was of there not being a huge amount of people in the room. He had heard no footsteps beyond that of the woman and the priest's girlfriend, apparently. Three humans, including the incapacitated priest – a couple of weak females, probably armed with stakes and holy water. That was no problem for someone as powerful as Victor Rothenstein! He almost laughed in delight. This was going to be easy!

"So. Your answer? Do I release you under the terms I mentioned?" Jackie persisted.

Victor grinned, allowing time to pass as if he was seriously contemplating the agreement. In reality, his intention was to rattle Jackie Nixon's confidence.

It worked. Impatiently, Jackie seethed, "Make your mind up."

Victor allowed another few seconds to go by, smiling as he counted them passing.

"What is your answer?" Jackie yelled.

"Open Sesame," Victor declared.

Her teeth gritted in annoyance, Jackie removed a pair of metal snips from her handbag and clipped at the silver wire around the fridge, the broken coils dropping to the floor. With some force, the door was flung open from the inside, knocking Jackie sprawling sideways onto the concrete floor, and Victor stepped out of his prison, fangs exposed, eyes wild, hissing his displeasure.

"You whore! Who are you to command me?" he roared, looming over Jackie.

"Kate!" cried Jackie, scrambling up.

Kate stepped forward, both arms straight in front of her, the small silver pistol aimed directly at Victor Rothenstein's heart, and said, "Hold it, punk! Silver bullets!"

Victor recoiled, hissing.

"Surely you don't think we're *that* stupid!" sneered Jackie, dusting herself down.

Rothenstein turned his attention back to Jackie. "Who are you, anyway, bitch?"

"If it matters... my father loved you like a brother, so I guess that makes me practically your niece!"

Rothenstein's brow furrowed. He clearly had no idea what she meant.

"I'm Jackie Nixon by marriage. You'd know me as Jaclyn Pinkman."

Victor gave out a huge hiss, his mind whirring. She had left Melas years ago, when she was a young teenager. Walter rarely ever spoke of personal issues – his mind always turned to his research and the daily tasks he performed for Victor. It was easy to forget he ever had a daughter. What did she know? What arcane knowledge had her father passed onto her? This, he hadn't anticipated. Victor's brain was reeling.

William, too, had momentarily paused in his endeavors, amazed. *Pinkman? Holy shit!*

"So. Call it a debt paid for my father's loyalty to you, in serving you with legal matters... accounts... anything that would have involved exposure to the sunlight. Hah! A simple deal," Jackie went on. "Your freedom, in exchange for some of your blood for myself... and for Kate."

Kate? William's head spun round to view Kate. He stared at her accusingly. Her own gaze was turned determinedly towards Jackie.

"Who is Kate?" asked Rothenstein.

"Questions, questions!" Jackie exploded. "I think you'll find that I'm the one calling the shots this time, Rothenstein. But – if it matters – Kate is my daughter."

"That's right," Kate took another step forward, keeping her gun trained on her target.

"Kate!" William gasped, staring at Kate, but she didn't flinch, still aiming the pistol at Rothenstein with a practiced steadiness that unnerved William even more, if that was possible. This was certainly not the Kate he knew. The Kate he had fallen in love with. That Kate was clearly a pretense – a complete fabrication. William's blood chilled: he was so utterly on his own against these people that he almost sympathized with Rothenstein.

"The only reason we didn't kill and drain your ass from the beginning, is so that the ritual remains precise and all the elements intact for the Release of the Darkness. I'm not a risk-taker. In that respect, anyway."

CHAPTER 26

The Release of the Darkness? Was that what Lucy had warned Alison about? The end of the world? From somewhere within the confines of the basement wall, Alison was listening to everything. She struggled to resurface from the gloopy suspension that entrapped her, getting nowhere. What the hell was this? If only she could get out, she might be able to do something!

Lucy had said she was the only one who could help! And somewhere in the background of low moans and faraway shrieks, she could hear a baby crying, very distantly. Alison listened hard. She couldn't quite make out if the baby sound was coming from within the walls, like the other tortured souls, or in the basement. Or somewhere else.

She tried to re-orientate herself. If she had fallen into the wall on her right hand side as she stood at the top of the basement staircase, then up behind her – and to the right, was the first floor of the house itself.

Was there a baby in there?

***

Victor Rothenstein seethed at Jackie's words. *The Release of the Darkness!*

This fucking woman was unbelievable! He was being used in more ways than one, and he was in no way comfortable with that. He was the one in control! This abasement went completely against his nature.

If this woman was so aware of the rituals of immortality and the Release of the Darkness, then Pinkman had clearly had more contact with his daughter after she'd left Melas than Victor realized. She had evidently received instruction from Pinkman or someone else. Satan only knew what knowledge she had.

For all I know, Pinkman might have told her everything! Victor would have to be cunning in his approach, he could see. He quickly gathered his thoughts, composing himself to develop a plan. He sneered at the small silver pistol Kate still held, but continued keeping his distance, nonetheless.

"Wait. Just what the hell do I have to do with any of this?" William piped up. He just couldn't come to terms with the fact that his girlfriend was actually Jackie's daughter, Kate Nixon. She'd been working with her mother all this while to trap Victor? Why did they need him?

"The priest-child speaks," Victor scoffed, relieved that a distraction had presented itself, giving him more time to perfect his next move. But the very presence of William gave him a new angle.

William persisted, "What was… all that, Kate?" He looked at her, imploringly, demanding a reason. "What have you done?"

"Will – I'm sorry, but…" she said, repressing a flicker of regret and ensuring that she finished her sentence firmly, devoid of emotion. "We needed you here."

"But... when we met... and we got together... did you *ever* care?" he asked. "I really loved you. If I can just understand... I still love you."

Kate's mask slipped a little, the pistol trembling in her hands.

"Oh, shit! My heart bleeds!" Jackie interjected. "For fuck's sake, get over yourself. Kate's job was to seduce you so you'd come along on the vampire hunt! You've fought Victor Rothenstein before and won. We *might* have needed you. Turns out – we don't!"

Kate pressed her lips together tightly and turned her focus solely to aiming the pistol on Victor again.

"In fact, Kate, you could shoot the boy here and now, since he has served his purpose," smiled Jackie.

Kate's face dropped, but before anyone else could react, of all people, Rothenstein's voice boomed out first: "NO!"

All eyes turned to him, in surprise.

"We have a deal. I agree to the blood transfer, IF I get to kill the priest and satiate myself on his blood!"

"No!" Kate gave an involuntary shriek of alarm, the pistol jerking in her hand.

Despite her best efforts to be objective and impassive; despite her trying to conceal the fact, Kate was still in love with William. Difficult as it would be to shoot him on her mother's command, it would have been better to shoot him in the arm or in some inconsequential and non-fatal place than allow Victor Rothenstein to drain him to a lifeless corpse.

"Kate!" snapped her mother, glaring at her daughter. "This is no time to be sentimental! We brought him into this to serve only one purpose." She turned her blonde head back to Rothenstein and addressed him levelly: "It's a deal. You bite us and stay to participate in the ritual – and you get to kill the boy."

"I am somewhat thirsty now," Rothenstein's eyes gleamed, as he looked William up and down. "I need sustenance before I do as you ask."

"Not so fast," Kate stepped forward, the gun pointing straight at Rothenstein's chest.

"That's right, vampire," Jackie chimed in. "Do you take us for fools? *First*, you let us taste your blood. THEN you participate in the ritual and guide me in the Release of Darkness. FINALLY, you get the boy!"

Rothenstein hissed his distaste, but with silver bullets in the chamber of the gun trained upon him, he had no choice but to comply.

"As you... wish..." he snarled.

CHAPTER 27

Trapped within the wall, seemingly in another dimension, yet still able to hear everything in the basement, Alison knew she had to act fast.

Within moments, there would be three vampires to contend with. Alison was furiously trying to remember all that she had researched about the Madison House.

If she was to fulfil her destiny, as Lucy had intimated, and stop the terrible Release of the Darkness, she had to get out of this fucking jello wall!

What the hell was this – with its moaning and wailing? Her husband Don had been very cagey about the reconstruction, but had let slip that Jackie Nixon had some funny ideas and he had to get some special materials included that had been a pain in the ass to collect and incorporate…

Incorporate… she thought. *From the Latin: incorporatus, the past participle of incorporare: to embody, incarnate!*

Jackie Nixon had been using the bodies and souls of people to build her house! *Jesus!* Alison recollected the notes she had read in Walter Pinkman's study about the creation of soul stones – which captured the essence of a human – the soul, and held it in suspension after death.

Such stones could be utilized to provide powerful life energy for spells and rituals. Only one was necessary for most eventualities.

Holy shit! Alison had spotted hundreds of oily gleaming pebbles in the base of the stucco at basement and foundation level. She had thought they were some weird design, but... *Oh, my God!* They were soul stones! No wonder the very walls were shrieking with the voices of tormented souls. Hundreds, if not thousands of souls were held in these very walls.

What kind of horrifying power would these have, if used in this so-called Release of the Darkness ritual? It didn't bear thinking about. But now that she knew what she was dealing with, she might be able to find a way out of this entrapment.

Alison knew she would have to summon up the spells she had learned that might help her to escape – and then, she had to single-handedly deal with three vampires. If she wasn't fast enough, there would be worse evil unleashed, and then, she feared, all would be lost.

Alison's knowledge might be academic and theoretical, but it was vast, and now she had to take it out of her intellectual mind and act upon it. She had spent the last few weeks in earnest, reading and preparing, driven by the urgency of the house's completion and Lucy's warnings to gather information about Pinkman's research, and how to deal with whatever might happen in future.

Except the future was now.

***

235

Victor Rothenstein extended his neck to one side, his chin thrust out arrogantly, his hatred-filled eyes never leaving Jackie Nixon's. She in turn could barely conceal a smile, her teeth biting her bottom lip in lascivious anticipation. She stood only an arm's reach away from the dark figure of Rothenstein, but Kate still held the gun towards Victor's breast, despite her arms aching. It could not be long now before they achieved their goal. She could take a little more pain for her mother's sake, and after that, their worries would be over. *Eternal life!*

With all the performance of a ritual in itself, Victor, with his head still tipped sideways, extended one hand, with his long-nailed index finger raised. The fingernail was razor-sharp, and after presenting it to the small group of onlookers like a stage magician, he drew the sharp nail slowly across his throat, close to his carotid artery, a red line appearing, then dripping with blood.

Jackie gave one warning glance to Kate to ensure she was still covering her back, before stepping forward, close to the vampire, their eyes still locked together. She inhaled Victor's funky scent, her breasts brushing against his shirt, and she grabbed a handful of the cotton cloth to tug him down to a level where she could reach his throat. Still with a sneer of hatred on his face, Victor bent towards her, and like lovers in an intimate embrace, Jackie pressed her face into his neck. A loud hiss emanated from Rothenstein as he felt the first pull of her mouth, sucking the blood from his veins, yet he was surprised to find that he found it strangely pleasant, like a release. Orgasmic, but he needed to keep his wits about him. He knew what it was like to be a newly fanged vampire with a voracious appetite.

Kate and William stared open-mouthed, wondering what would happen next. After a couple of long seconds, it was Victor who violently pushed Jackie away, tenacious as she was, since she had apparently been feeding hungrily, almost unable to stop. She unwillingly drew away, hissing, her lips, cheeks and chin smeared with red, and her mouth dripping with blood. The characteristic elongated canines of a vampire were already apparent.

She turned towards Kate, with a look of triumph; grinning bloodily, her eyes now glowing red. "Now, you, Kate!" she commanded.

Kate glanced quickly towards William, who lay still on the floor, horror-stricken, but she stepped forward, handing the silver pistol to her mother. If indeed, this vampire within the body of Jackie Nixon was still her mother.

Victor Rothenstein's mask of arrogance and hatred had slipped. He looked uneasy, slightly weakened, William thought. William took the opportunity to work on his chains, his eyes still watching the events before him, while his hands worked at their task.

Jackie took the gun and aimed it at Victor. "We're still not taking any risks, Rothenstein, so don't get any ideas. Drink deep, Kate. But not too deeply. We still need him for the next ritual."

Kate pressed herself up against Victor Rothenstein and stood on tiptoe, tugging at his blood-drenched collar to bring his gaping throat a little closer to her pink lips. Her mouth locked onto his throat, and he gave a heavy sigh, his eyes rolling up into his head, as she drank, sucking in a rhythm that mimicked his heartbeat. Both of them were lost in the moment.

"ENOUGH!" Jackie barked, her red eyes blazing. Already her skin had assumed the grayish pallor of a vampire, so her eyes burned like red-hot coals from her blood-leached face.

"Aaaaaahhhh!" Kate expressed an angry cry as Victor pushed her off, helped by Jackie Nixon's dragging Kate's head away by a fistful of her blonde hair.

Kate spun around, her eyes glowing spitefully, the whole bottom half of her face covered in thick blood. She had gorged for the couple of seconds she had had, but she wanted more.

"Why do you STOP ME?" she roared, crazed with blood-lust.

Jackie slapped her firmly across her bloody face, causing her to stagger sideways.

"You know why, fool!" cried Jackie. "For the ritual itself!"

Victor stood, bowed over slightly, one hand clamped to his throat. He looked disheveled and dazed, and if possible, even paler than usual: his complexion was a grisly, cadaverous color.

"Fetch the child!" Jackie commanded Kate.

William stopped abruptly, his head swivelling in alarm. *Child?*

Kate wiped the back of her hand across her face, smearing and transferring blood further across her arm. "No!" she responded.

Jackie gave a roar, the force of which blew Kate's hair back like a strong wind, causing her to squint her eyes shut. "This is not the time for childish fucking antics!"

Jackie pushed past her daughter, flinging out an arm that sent Kate flying twelve feet through the air and landing in a crumpled heap on the concrete floor. Unconcerned about her daughter's welfare, Jackie determinedly marched towards the basement steps and ran up them lightly.

William couldn't help wincing in concern, watching his girlfriend's body thrown like a rag doll and hearing the crack of bones as it hit the hard surface. He still couldn't shut off his feelings for Kate, whoever she was now. His heart involuntarily gave a flip of relief when she immediately recovered, hissing her displeasure and standing up, brushing off the plaster dust from her clothing.

Victor himself had slumped with exhaustion and slid down the closed refrigerator door, where he sat, gasping in shallow breaths.

William worked at his chains, frustrated. He had managed to gradually ease his way, unseen, towards the metal snips Jackie had discarded when she released Rothenstein from the silver wire.

Ever since, William had been subtly fretting away at the thick chain that bound his wrists with the sharp but barely effectual blades. The small metal cutters were designed for thick wire, not chain links of the weight binding him, so they were chewing their way through slower than a fret saw would.

And that was only when he was sure the attention of the others – now all vampires – was not on him. Whenever they looked towards him, he had to otherwise conceal all sight of the metal snips in the folds of his now grubby and bloodied cassock. They were making some headway with biting through the metal, he knew, but painfully slowly. He just wasn't sure he would release himself in time to do any good at all. All by himself against three vampires, along with the potential Release of the Darkness, whatever that was? It didn't sound good.

***

Alison was thinking the same thing. She had tried a number of incantations, but so far, to no avail – she had not yet escaped. She had, however, through some chance and magic, managed to work her way to the surface of the basement wall. She found that she must have sunk to the floor level, but thankfully no farther, since she was no longer at the top of the basement steps, but could now clearly see the others in the room, as if through an impermeable membrane. She pressed her hands against the wall, but even though it appeared transparent, the surface felt rubbery and had no give at all. And evidently, like a one-way mirror, no one in the basement could see her, even though she could see through it like glass. She hesitated to go any further in her attempts to escape while Jackie strode purposefully past her, oblivious, so close by she could have touched her, if only this barrier weren't in the way. Now that she could see the lay of the land, she paused for thought.

For the moment it might be best that she remain concealed within the wall, unseen. She could now see William on the floor, his hands and feet wrapped in chains. If she could get him free to help her, she would have an ally! But would magic work through the wall between them, or would she have to free herself first and act fast to release him? Two humans – both adept in different ways at fighting vampires – against one strong, established vampire, and two newly turned. Surely the odds were better now?

Besides, at the moment, Victor Rothenstein looked pathetic. And Jackie was out of the basement. Maybe Alison should take action now, while only Kate remained?

CHAPTER 28

"If it's any consolation," Kate said, approaching William, who hurriedly sank his bound hands between his knees to conceal the metal snips, "I did love you."

"Ha!" William said bitterly, only wanting her to go away and leave him to his own metal-clipping devices. But in the meantime, while she still had some vestige of humanity remaining, he asked, "What child was she talking about?"

Kate's pale lips tightened into a thin line on her chalky face, her red eyes glowing.

But before she could answer or not, the sound of a baby crying came to their attention, followed by the clip of Jackie's heels down the steps and across the concrete until she came within William's eye-line, holding a large, several months-old baby wrapped in a black silk blanket.

At the sound, Victor Rothenstein, as if revived, stood up. "Is that the Harker brat?"

"What?" William cried, struggling against his chains more frantically.

Jackie laughed, a crone-like, sinister laugh. "Isn't it a beautiful irony? Jonathan Harker, the vampire-killer's baby son, killed by vampires?" Her shrieks of delight echoed around the room.

William roared in rage, and wrestled himself onto his feet, still bound by chains. In one swift bound, Rothenstein leapt across the room and pushed William over, where he fell heavily on his already bruised elbow. William yelped in pain, still struggling to get up, but Rothenstein placed his foot firmly on William's neck.

Rothenstein snarled, "Let me kill the bastard now!"

"No!" snapped Jackie. "Make him watch!"

Rothenstein bent down, grabbing William by the back of his neck, and forced him into a sitting position, holding him in place with a vice-like grip despite his body bucking, and his heavily chained limbs thrashing as he yelled expletives, demanding them to let him go and stop whatever they were about to do.

"Stop! You fucking bastards!"

The baby too, was screaming by now, but Jackie laid him down on a low platform and unwrapped the black silk that enfolded the small child. Beneath the covering, the child was naked, and his innocent vulnerability struck William even deeper.

"NOOOOO!" William shouted, still struggling, his strength almost inhuman against the heavy chains, but still no match for the inhuman Victor Rothenstein and his deathlike grasp.

The child remained on his back, kicking and waving his fists, his face bright red and eyes screwed tight with incessant screaming. The black silk had fallen off the child and draped over the platform on which he lay, like an altar cloth.

"SHUT THE FUCK UP!" Jackie screeched, her snarling, red-eyed gray face thrust close up into the baby's face. Terrified, the baby silenced itself, paralyzed in fear, its bunched hands trembling in mid-air.

"Hold its head, Kate, and if it starts that shrieking again, put your hand over its mouth."

Kate made to move forward but glanced at William, her pace stuttering, before she did as she was told, clamping her hands around the child's petrified face. The baby boy began to whimper.

"Jesus! The quicker the better!" Jackie muttered, raising a jeweled dagger high above her head, and beginning to mutter some indistinguishable words under her breath.

"NOOOOOO!" screamed William, but Victor Rothenstein squeezed the back of his neck a little more, and he felt himself unable to speak or move, although he could still see, only too well.

Jackie Nixon, after murmuring an incantation, plunged the blade of the dagger deep into the baby's chest wall, shouting, "TO SATAN!"

The small child gave a blood-curdling scream of pain, and began to cry heart-wrenching, wracking sobs that only served to pump more blood out of the wound in rhythmic gushes.

William opened his mouth to screech in protest, but with Rothenstein still gripping his neck, no sound came out. He felt as if his own heart was bursting; broken.

Kate had stepped back a few paces, her hands held up with the fingers still frozen in the same position they had been to hold the baby's face, staring in horror.

But worse was to come. With the blade of the knife, Jackie carved a slit in the still-living baby's chest, peeling back the skin with its thin rim of pale fat and red flesh, and plunged her hands into the warm, bloody body. She thrust her fingers between the baby's ribs and with one strong yank, she ripped out his ribcage, the greenstick bones snapping like twigs with flaps of delicate young muscle, flesh and skin clinging to them like tattered rags as she tossed the framework of bones aside. The baby gave one agonized gurgling scream, and then thankfully lost consciousness, although his heart was miraculously still beating, blood still pulsating out of the bloody mass.

Jackie gripped the small beating heart in her fingers, feeling it flutter like a frightened bird, before she wrenched it out from the arteries and veins that held it, blood spattering out all over her face. Lizard-like, her tongue shot out and she licked around to capture the drops that had landed on her cheeks, lips and chin.

William almost passed out, unable to bear the sight of his tiny cousin's now dead body a pulpy mass of gore, with a vampire holding his tiny heart dripping blood from her vicious fist. His stomach roiled and pitched like a boat tossed on a stormy sea, and he fought to swallow down the vomit that lurched up from the back of his throat.

But Rothenstein still held him, and he had little control over his own body. A paroxysm overtook him, unstoppable. Boiling hot, acidic vomit shot up through his nose, spraying out of his burning nostrils and mouth in a flaming fountain. Victor Rothenstein dropped his hold and stepped back in distaste, as William retched up a bucketful of puke, acrid with the stench of bile, old food, and stomach acid. For the next several minutes, William lay immobile on his side in his own vomit, and retched and retched, unable to stop.

Jackie did not flinch. Holding the tiny heart, still dripping blood, she turned to the wall behind the black altar and began using the heart to paint on its plastered surface. Once she had bent and smeared a short vertical line from the floor, she turned back to the baby's dead body and dipped the heart back into the puddle of blood that remained pooled in its chest cavity, bringing her dripping fist out again and swinging around again to the wall, continuing to extend the line in a macabre bloody outline that appeared to be created from her own febrile imagination.

But she had a specific design in mind.

CHAPTER 29

Throughout this horrific process, Alison had been struggling, first to send the intent of the magical spells she had memorized straight through the rubbery membrane, in an attempt to release William's shackles. But it was as if she was in a different dimension, and the spells bounced back against this weird, transparent but immutable barrier.

The only good thing to come from this, was that she felt more powerful herself – the release, freedom and strength she had been trying to project through the rubbery wall had been mirrored back towards herself.

She could only thank the Lord that she hadn't sent any evil intent through, although the first thing she had ever learned, in her youth, about wiccan magic was that any black magic and evil intent sent would be returned to the sender, the evil increased thrice-fold, and would make the practitioner suffer far worse than their intended victim.

So when Alison witnessed the terrible sacrifice of the baby, she was strong enough to accept it. Although she was appalled, it did not reduce her to a gibbering emotional wreck, as it would have done before she had thrown some strengthening spells out that had hit her back, without reaching William. Therefore, although her intention had been to hopefully save the baby by releasing William, she had an inner knowing that her next attempts to break through the wall would be successful. She had got closer to a breakthrough all the time, and had unwittingly managed to empower herself even more, which could only help to overthrow the vampires in the long run.

Obsessively focused and unaware of anything else, Jackie was still using the tiny baby's heart as a paintbrush, dipping it into the pool of blood and painting on the basement wall, following a previously pencil-sketched outline of an arched doorway. Kate and Victor Rothenstein, knowing that the time was near, had approached her too, and stood behind Jackie on either side of the bloody doorway that was now taking shape before their eyes.

Recovering his wits and stomach, William cast his eyes around for the metal snips that had clattered to the floor in the affray. Even more urgently, he needed to escape: he had nothing to lose now that Jonathan and Amanda's baby was dead for sure, and he wanted revenge so badly, it hurt. This was personal. Since Rothenstein and Kate had stepped forward to join Jackie, and were gazing with awe at her painting, William knew there was no better time to make the metal cutter's blades fret away at the chain links. He had already managed to get specific links halfway broken, at both his ankles and his wrists. While the vampires were distracted, he had his best chance to saw away at the metal further still, and this time he was driven by almost mindless fury. He didn't care if he died trying, but if he could free himself, he would smash those vampire bastards to a pulp. Except perhaps for Kate. But he knew he would even have to stake her, too, much as it pained him to think of it.

As Jackie painted in the last bloody smear of the outline that joined the rest of the painted line to the ground, she stepped back away from her work and the whole jagged bloody doorway began to pulsate with a red glow.

Kate gave a little gasp, but all three vampires stared at the doorway and began to chant together: *"Locos Umbrae Regnans Satan! Agite Tenebrae Abyssi.."*

William winced, as in his haste to clip the metal around his wrists, he caught the skin.

"To Teikhos Dierzasthô! To sumbolaion diakonêtô moi..."

Within the wall of the basement steps behind them, caught amongst the soul stones, Alison knew she was so close to release, it would take only another few minutes of chanting a release spell, and she would be free. She increased her own focus, as she heard the increasing volume of the three vampires in their invocation of the Darkness:

"Pareo pactum quod servo mihi. Doru Petras!"

The doorway outline, after its glowing, had already begun to recede into a blackness that began to take the shape of a cavernous open doorway. *The door to the Darkness!*

"Agite Tenebrae Abyssi!" cried Jackie, her arms raised aloft, facing the shadowy shape in the wall. Rothenstein and Kate echoed her words and movement.

With a great whooshing sound, a powerful gust of wind and a shaking of the foundations of the house that almost knocked the vampires off their feet, the wall contained within the doorway shape dissolved into a black hole, almost palpable in its darkness, inside which they could see pale shadows shifting slowly, as graceful as smoke. From somewhere deep inside, behind the gray spirit forms, was the sound of wailing and moaning: almost musical to the vampires' ears.

As if entranced, her eyes wide and blazing red, her lips curled in a smile of wonderment, Jackie stepped immediately through the doorway and into the Darkness. She turned, expectantly, and Kate, almost hypnotically motivated, since she moved unconsciously, followed her mother across the threshold. Rothenstein however, remained in the basement.

"Victor!" called Jackie, her voice echoing as if down a distant corridor. "Come!"

But Victor stayed exactly where he was, his hands still raised in the air, as if frozen after the ritual. But Jackie's voice had now broken the spell and he dropped his hands, calling back: "I have a task to do, still… Some important unfinished business to get rid of!"

He swung around, a smug and arrogant grin on his face, prepared to finish William off for good.

He gasped in shock. On the floor where William had been sitting not five minutes earlier, there lay only the chains that had bound him. Before Rothenstein could close his gaping mouth and cast his eyes around the room, a body suddenly flew at him, searing his cheek by pressing something against his face with the intensity of a branding iron.

It was Alison. The final invocation that had shaken the very foundations of the house and opened up the doorway in the wall had released her, too, permitting her releasing spells to work even more effectively because the structure of the soul house was made unsound at the very moment in which the doorway to the Darkness opened. She, in turn, had managed to facilitate William's freedom from his chains, too, since they gave way with one tug of her supercharged hands.

"Come on!" she'd whispered, while the vampires were concentrating on the doorway. Immediately, she and William had taken cover in the shadows, from where she had flown at Rothenstein's face, crucifix in hand, as soon as he had turned around.

"Fucking bastard!" she yelled, thrusting the cross into his face.

Rothenstein's pale skin blistered with a hissing sound beneath the wood of the cross, and the smell of burning flesh filled Alison's nostrils as she clung to his neck, forcing the cross deeper, searing into his cheekbone.

With a roar, Kate flew out of the portal, grabbed Alison by the hair and wrenched her off Rothenstein, before leaping upon her and wrestling her to the ground. The wooden cross Alison had been holding had been knocked from her hand and skittered across the concrete floor in the fray.

Only newly blood-initiated into the vampire family, Kate's superhuman strength had not yet reached its peak, but ironically, Alison's human strength had grown, owing to the power of the spells she had cast bouncing back at her while she was trapped within the impenetrable wall. So Alison was, for the moment at least, a match for Kate.

Alison held Kate off at arm's length, her hand clawed around the vampire's throat, while Kate's eyes flamed venomously, her fangs bared and hungrily drooling saliva. Both arms waving, her fingernails slashed ineffectually but with great violence, dangerously close to Alison's eyes.

William took his opportunity. He was less keen to kill Rothenstein or help Alison than to tear Jackie Nixon apart limb from limb, just as she had tragically done to his baby cousin. So he was already at the threshold of the Darkness, ready to step beyond, when Rothenstein noticed where he was and threw himself upon him, whipping William's legs from underneath him and rolling him over onto his back.

Then Kate screamed, as blood began to drip from her neck, spattering the concrete floor. She whipped around, Alison hanging from her neck with a knife in her hand, evidently trying to saw off Kate's head where she stood.

"Stupid bitch!" screeched Kate, only mildly distracted. Annoyed, she reached around, grabbed Alison's head by her hair, swung her body forward and sent it flying through the air where it hit the wall, her ribs cracking so she was momentarily winded and immobilized. But Kate immediately threw herself on Alison and within a flash, the two women were back on their feet, still apparently fighting to the death. Clumps of hair flew and blood spattered from slashing nails, violent punches to mouths, and Alison's teeth, but Kate had still not managed to get her fangs near Alison.

Kate got Alison in a tight headlock, and was just trying to figure out how she could fang the bitch even though Alison's throat was completely enclosed within the crook of her arm. Kate squeezed, since throttling Alison unconscious and then drinking her dry seemed her best bet, given the way she was fighting back. They staggered together, locked in a ball of flailing fists and feet, lurching unsteadily towards the doorway.

CHAPTER 30

William and Rothenstein were engaged in their own battle. They wrestled for a second, but not only was Rothenstein a strong man against a barely out of teen age boy, but he was also a vampire with superhuman strength.

"Stop struggling!" hissed Rothenstein, but William summoned up all the strength he had from his bruised limbs in an attempt to fend him off. He managed to get a hand to Rothenstein's chin, and had locked his elbow straight.

"Idiot!" Rothenstein seethed, with his eyes wide and threatening. "Then we'll do this my way!"

He wrenched William's arm free and tore his collar away from his throat, exposing his temptingly soft skin, with the promise of veins and arteries beneath. Rothenstein's thin mouth opened in a sinister grimace, his lips peeling back to expose his vampiric canines, drooling in anticipation of gorging on William's warm, young blood. He bent his head towards him, eyes burning red.

Still doubled over in Kate's strong headlock, Allison was already reaching for the stake in her cargo pants pocket but she couldn't quite reach the mallet she had hanging from her tool belt, because her other hand was digging her fingernails hard into Kate's arm, trying to loosen her stranglehold. Overbalancing, they both staggered, still fighting, and lurched over the doorway threshold. Together, they fell through the Darkness portal, Alison giving a blood-curdling scream, leaving Victor and William alone in the room.

Victor froze, crimson eyes wide, then suddenly pulled William up into a sitting position and spoke to him earnestly, in a low voice: "Play along, and you won't get hurt."

"W… what?" William stuttered, amazed, as he felt Victor's hold on him loosen.

Victor continued: "I can't fucking believe this. This woman's nuts! NOBODY fucks with me the way she did and gets away with it."

William frowned, still uncertain what was going on here, but he listened intently to Victor's torrent of words.

"Hell, she has NO FUCKING CLUE the forces she is unleashing!" He stopped for a brief moment, gazing into space with a look of terror, as if reflecting upon the horrifying outcome of Jackie's actions. "At least I knew my place in the grand order of things. I studied the forces, but I never tried to take the throne!"

***

Within the Darkness, Alison was completely blind. All was utterly black and she had no idea of where she was in relation to anything else, but she still had a hold of Kate in a vice-like grip. She dared not let go, since then she would have no concept at all of where her enemy was.

All she could do was keep clinging onto Kate with one hand as she had done when they fell. At least if she kept her within her grasp, she would still have a clue, so she wasn't taken by surprise.

She flailed out her other hand, slashing blindly with the stake she clutched, sometimes striking something solid, but always ineffectually. Kate's body seemed sometimes close, sometimes at arm's length, but whenever Alison thrust the stake, it hit dense air or sideswiped Kate.

It was like fighting under a heavy cloak of thick cloth, her movements muffled and restricted. The blackness was bad enough, but the atmosphere here was almost as dense as when she was trapped inside the wall. Worse still, was the fact that she was tiring – the doom-laden evil surrounding her seemed to be draining her of any strength she had left. And somewhere, dangerously within striking distance, Kate was preparing to kill her, the vampire's strength increasing the more hers depleted.

Alison felt strong fingers scrabbling into her scalp, clutching her hair hard and winding it into a fist, then the scorching pain of her hair being ripped out by the roots as her head was violently yanked back with an excruciating crack.

That was the last she knew.

***

"Throne?" William asked, but Victor was too absorbed to hear him, let alone explain.

But as if snapped back to the present by the sound of William's voice, Victor turned his attention back to him, snarling, "That crazy bitch! She's going to drag us all to hell!"

"Then why are you helping her?" William asked.

"I wanted to see how much she knew. Call it intellectual curiosity, if you like. I didn't think she would get so far... do so much."

Victor's eyes flashed with pure hatred. "I was also under duress. If you recall, her bitch daughter held a gun to my head. But..." His gaze flicked in an instant towards the portal nearby and then he hissed quietly, "Wait. Here she comes!"

Rothenstein drew William closer as if to sink his fangs into his throat and whispered, "I'm leaving you alive because we may need to work together to get out of this."

"And if I refuse?" William started to protest.

Kate re-emerged from the portal with the silver pistol drawn.

Suddenly, the weight of Rothenstein's looming body was completely off William. The vampire had been flung violently aside. Through half-closed eyes, William looked up in wonder.

Dazed with surprise, William saw Kate standing above him, blood dripping from her mouth, her pistol trained on Rothenstein, the other hand jauntily placed on her hip.

"I guess I'm dumb," she shrugged. "I keep letting my heart dictate my actions." She turned to Rothenstein, who lay a few feet away, struggling to sit up, his mouth twisted in a mask of anger.

"You killed my boyfriend, you bastard. That was my prerogative. But besides, I could have turned him!"

William remained slumped on the floor.

Kate barked, "I've still got the gun and silver bullets, Rothenstein! If only Mother didn't need you as a guide in the Darkness, I wouldn't hesitate to blast you there myself, bloodsucker. But step out of line again, and I will!"

Rothenstein glared at her as he got to his feet.

"Now, where were we?" Kate said. "Oh, yeah. What can I say? When Mother's done with you, we'll be fighting over who tortures you first! But for now, get in there!"

She beckoned Rothenstein towards the portal with a jerk of the gun barrel and he reluctantly obeyed, glaring at Kate with his lip curled, seething with hatred. Both of the vampires stepped into the doorway, but in a sudden movement, Rothenstein grabbed William, wrenching him up by the arm, sinking his face towards his throat and muttering, "Play dead!" before he dragged him through the portal into the Darkness along with them.

It truly was Darkness, a tangible blackness, which felt like dense velvet smothering all that it embraced, but to William it seemed to permeate inside his body, too; filling his whole self – even his soul – with a real and palpably unpleasant unease. William felt himself dropped from Rothenstein's clutches, and had a sense of unaccountable loss and terrible solitude. It was as if he had lost his only link to reality.

The portal shut behind them with a strange metallic clang.

William shook his head in disbelief. *What the fuck?*

Disoriented, he had no sense of space of time; no idea of whether he was sitting or hanging in mid-air, only a suffocating sensation of great evil seeping through his skin, an awareness of impending doom, and the background of ghostly howling and groaning all around his ears. The noise was chilling enough, but accompanied by the sensation of evil that he felt all around and inside him – William was appalled.

Beside him where he lay on the ground – if indeed, there was a ground – there was something solid, but soft. He dabbed his fingers around in the blackness, and they touched some fabric. It felt like clothing, and then as he pressed his fingers deeper and wider – a limb. A person? A body? Whatever or whoever it was, there was no movement. No sign of life. His fingers exploring further, he found the shape of a mallet, attached to... a tool belt. Alison.

As if someone had turned on a light switch, a dim red wash of light was suddenly thrown onto William's surroundings, and figures became half-visible to him. Sure enough, Alison's corpse lay next to him, her head cocked at an unnatural angle, her neck obviously broken, with a gaping gash in it like a parody of a grin.

Standing above William and staring at Kate, was a grim-faced Rothenstein, red eyes blazing with fury.

In the Darkness, where William still lay, pretending to be dead next to the drained, twisted corpse of Alison Smith, he was shocked to witness a flurry of gray disembodied hands fall upon the imposing figure of

Victor Rothenstein, who hissed and cried out in protest.

"What the hell's this?" he roared, his powerful body rearing back, and his eyes blazing still more vermilion in the dim red light of the Darkness.

He struggled hard, but was held firm by those steely hands.

To his horror, a heavily studded collar was violently clipped around his neck, attached to a long chain leash held taut in unseen hands. The vampire gave out a loud, low growl of protest at the realization and the indignity of it all. "Fuck you, bitch!"

"I think you mean 'Fuck you, Your Majesty!'" Jackie Nixon's voice sneered.

Her next words were suddenly roared out with such thunderous loudness that the whole of the Darkness quaked: the very atmosphere vibrated.

"BOW, you serf! Bow down to the MOTHER OF DARKNESS – QUEEN OF THE VAMPIRES!"

EPILOGUE

Back in the basement at the other side of the Darkness, gradually, the doorway again became first simply a cavernous black hole, then a two-dimensional shaded shape on the wall, then an outline painted in blood, then an imperceptible pencil line, and finally, a clean, newly plastered whitewashed wall. It was pristine and pure.

As the entrance to the Darkness became a normal wall again, the tiny ragged corpse of the baby on the black silk-shrouded platform was crumpling even further, its small blood-drenched arms and chubby, dimpled legs crumpling, and the spattered dome of its skull shrinking down like a deflating balloon.

The body was dissolving, and even the blood was seemingly being drunk down by the very surfaces it touched. The baby's tiny scraps of remaining flesh, blood, skin, muscle and bone that had been flung around the room, too, were disappearing, sucked through the concrete and into the earthy foundations.

The fragile broken ribcage where it lay on the concrete after being savagely ripped asunder and carelessly tossed aside, and the poor, abused heart, with its delicate membrane viciously rubbed away on the wall and the muscle raw and shredded, exposing the tiny chambers – all were gradually being absorbed into the floor. They were being subsumed into the substance of the house itself, every drop, leaving no trace or evidence whatsoever. They, too, had become incorporated into the Soul House.

All was silent, clean and white. Waiting.

A short while later, Donovan Smith rang the front doorbell of the Madison House, but no one answered. Jackie's car was parked outside, so he could only assume that she was still someplace inside the mansion. Don entered with his own key, calling her name and surprised to hear no response. He began looking for her, stepping into the lavishly sized living room, but finding it echoingly empty. The basement door at the end of the hallway was wide open, so he ran down the steps, curious.

"Jackie?" he called, walking around the empty basement, seeing only the workmen's remaining tools propped up against the wall with the spattered paint cans and sack of plaster. There was a pile of chains lying on the ground near the platform she had unaccountably requested that they build into the floor. He could see that Jackie had draped also some kind of black, silky-satin sheet on the platform itself.

Kinky! he thought in surprise. Jackie usually liked straight sex, which, frankly, he was finding boring. His own wife was becoming increasingly more attractive to him, and he could hardly wait for this job to finish. Then maybe he could stop prostituting himself and get back to normal.

. Satisfied that Jackie wasn't hiding, naked, in the shadows, Don went up the steps, puzzled. He searched the rest of the house, switching on lights and peering into the bedrooms and bathrooms, but found no one. He rang her cell phone. It went straight to voicemail, but he didn't bother leaving a message, simply clicking off the call and cursing under his breath.

Leaving the house, he switched on his small Maglite to scan the beam across the garden, but there was nobody there, either.

Finally, he decided he might as well go home to Alison.

It would actually be good to see her.

ABOUT THE AUTHOR

Gary Lee Vincent was born in 1974, in Clarksburg, West Virginia, where he lives with his wife Carla and daughter Amber Lee. He is a graduate of Fairmont State University and Columbus University. Vincent holds a Ph.D. and M.S. in Computer Information Systems and a B.S. in Business Administration Management and Psychology.

He is a real estate developer, entrepreneur, author and recording artist.

His interests include music, travel, photography, technology, art, and of course, creative writing.

ALSO BY
GARY LEE VINCENT

WWW.GARYLEEVINCENT.COM

When an archaeological dig goes horribly wrong, the team is trapped in an alternate world where evil awaits them at every turn. Find out who will survive the Passageway! Skeleton warriors, zombies, other undead beings and werewolves are all very real inside the Passageway! Embark on a deadly tale that will keep you guessing which path to take as you descend into madness in Gary Lee Vincent's bizarro tribute to H.P. Lovecraft. Passageway will leave you breathless to the end!

www.GaryVincent.com   **Burning Bulb**

GARY LEE VINCENT'S
DARKENED
THE WEST VIRGINIA VAMPIRE SERIES

DARKENED WATERS

When the world goes to hell, the chosen must arise!

As Talman Cane orchestrates a flood of epic proportions in this third installment of the *Darkened* series the towns of Melas and Tarklin are caught completely off guard by the deluge. Hell-bent on finishing what they started, the evil brothers return to the lunatic asylum to take care of the witnesses and add to the ever-growing army of the undead.

Aided by Lucifer himself and the insane vampire demon Legion, the stage is set to channel all of the forces of hell to come forth. In an all-out race to survive, Jonathan, William, and Amanda soon discover they are up against impossible odds as Lucifer opens the Gateway to Hell, ushering in the zombie apocalypse and the End Times.

Find out who will survive this cosmic battle of the ages in *Darkened Waters!*

DARKENED SOULS

Melas and the Madison House are about to be rebuilt.
True evil is about to be reborne!

Young ex-priest and vampire-killer William is drawn back to the West Virginian town that almost killed him, where his vampire arch-enemy Victor Rothenstein still stalks the earth.

The town of Melas lies destroyed after the battle of the End of Days. But why is wealthy Jackie Nixon so eager to rebuild it using the bone dust of murdered souls?

Terrible evil has visited before, but the Gateway to Hell is about to be reopened in a horrific climax. And this time – it's personal.

WWW.DARKENEDHILLS.COM

Burning Bulb
PUBLISHING

THE TAILSMAN

From the creators of *The Big Book of Bizarro* and *Westward Hoes* comes a new comic unlike anything you have ever seen!

He's hot on the trail, looking for some *tail*...

Sly Franko was a man of the West, a forger of the wild frontier. Like the Country Western song that would be written years after he died, the words, "Faster horses, younger women, and more money," seemed to be the anthem of this horn dog cowboy.

Franko would ride into town on a blazing saddle, find the closest saloon to wet the whistle, belly up to a good card game, and find him a hot-loving hussy to get his cowpoke on with.

However, Sly might have met his match when a visit to bathroom leads to terror and death. Can Sly and his poker buddies solve the mystery before more of the townsfolk are murdered? Find out in this exciting premier issue of *The Tailsman*!

WWW.BURNINGBULBCOMICS.COM

ANTHOLOGIES
BIZARRO AND TRANSGRESSIVE FICTION

THE BIG BOOK OF BIZARRO

The Big Book of Bizarro brings together the peculiar prose of an international cast of the most grotesquely-gonzo, genre-grinding modern writers who ever put pen to paper (or mouse to pad), including:

NIGHT OF THE LIVING DEAD horror writers John Russo & George Kosana; HUSTLER MAGAZINE erotica contributors Eva Hore, Andrée Lachapelle, & J. Troy Seate and established Bizarro genre authors D. Harlan Wilson, William Pauley III, Wol-vriey, Laird Long, Richard Godwin and so many more!

From Alien abductions to Zombie sex, The Big Book of Bizarro contains OVER FIFTY STORIES of the most outrélandish transgressive fiction that you'll ever lay your capricious and curious hands upon!

WESTWARD HOES

Nine outlaw writers rode into town from obscurity to pen nine tantalizing tales of horror and fantasy, and leaving once they branded their own personal marks on the weird western genre and became living legends of the American Frontier experience.

Like drunken Indian scouts, the writers fervidly tracked down and captured the Western genre, tore off its fashionable veneer and ravished its exposed essence.

So belly up to the bar with your favorite soiled dove and enjoy perusing these thrilling tales of Old West debauchery, danger and desire; compiled by the publisher of The Big Book of Bizarro and featuring the bizarro novella *Big Trouble in Little Ass* by Wol-vriey.

Burning Bulb
PUBLISHING

RISE OF THE DEAD

AN EARTH-SHATTERING ANTHOLOGY OF ZOMBIE TERROR

Featuring Stories By:

John A. Russo   Tyson Blue   E.L. Stice   Nelson W. Pyles

Andy Rausch   Stephen Spignesi   R.D. Riley   Zakary McGaha

David J. Fairhead   Gary Lee Vincent   David C. Hayes   Rachel Montgomery

Paul Victor Wargelin   David F. Walker   William Vitka

Rich Bottles Jr.   Douglas Brode

RISE OF THE DEAD - a collection of seventeen tales of unspeakable zombie terror. Featuring a foreword and short story by John A. Russo and the short story *Cocaine Connie* by Gary Lee Vincent!

www.TheJohnRusso.com

Burning Bulb
PUBLISHING

WEST VIRGINIA-THEMED
HUMORROROTICA

BY RICH BOTTLES JR.

HELLHOLE WEST VIRGINIA

From the heights of Mothman's perch high atop the Silver Bridge in Point Pleasant to the depths of Hellhole Cavern in Pendleton County, evil lurks within the shadows as the sun sets upon the haunted hills and hollows of West Virginia.

Bizarro author Rich Bottles Jr. blows the coffin lid off horror genre clichés with this tour de force cast of Eco-friendly vampires, beach-yearning zombies and sex-starved she-devils.

LUMBERJACKED

If you are easily offended or do not possess a truly depraved sense of humor, this story may not be the light summer reading fare you desire. As for the four feisty female freshmen stranded on top of West Virginia's third highest mountain, they have no choice but to experience the sick, twisted debauchery and perverted mayhem described deep inside the tight unbroken bindings of this horrific missive.

Lumberjacked takes the reader to a nightmarish world where character development and aesthetic integrity are prematurely cut short by the swinging axes of maniacal lumberjacks, who are hell bent on death and destruction in the remote forests of Appalachia. And at the climax, when paranoia crosses over to the paranormal, Lumberjacked makes Deliverance look like a family raft trip down the Lower Gauley.

THE MANACLED

What happens when twin brothers lease out the former West Virginia State Penitentiary with the false purpose of filming a documentary on supernatural phenomena, but their true intention is to make a pornographic movie?

Chaos ensues as the disturbed spirits of murdered convicts, along with the reanimated dead from the neighboring Indian Burial Mound, take their vengeance on the unwary and undressed trespassers.

Zombies, ghosts, mobsters and porn collide in this bizarro tale from horror author Rich Bottles Jr.

Burning Bulb
PUBLISHING